I0745084

Number Twenty-four

Oliver Eade

www.olivereadebooks.org

Front cover artwork copyright © Fiona Ruiz 2019
Images of dogs from www.123rf.com

ISBN: 978-1-912513-53-6

Silver Quill Publishing

www.silverquillpublishing.com

Dedicated to
Bella

and to
Isla, Nick and Genevieve

Acknowledgements

I am indebted to Iona McGregor for her helpful comments and advice, and to others in Silver Quill Publishing for proofreading input. Also, I'm so grateful to my beloved wife, Yvonne Wei-Lun, for her seemingly limitless tolerance and understanding. It was bad enough for her to be married to a doctor during years of interrupted nights and medical moods and frowns, but to have this version of a husband replaced by a perpetually anguished writer would, for many women, have been the last straw. I also wish to thank writing colleagues, including those in the Borders Writers Forum and The Society of Medical Writers, for their gracious support over the years. Above all else, I am beholden to Man's best friend, the Dog, for inspiring this story.

*Whilst a woman called Victoria ruled the United Kingdom, mostly from her Palace of Buckingham in London, England, the Scottish Borders ruled itself, mostly from a town called Hawick. The fact that even in Scotland many did not know how to pronounce the hometown of Hawick folk ('Hawick' as in 'Boing'), didn't trouble them too much. They merely got on with their busy lives in the proud knowledge that her grey stone woollen mills, nestled in the valley of the River Teviot, played a major role in keeping humanity warm in the rest of the world. The rival Borders towns of Selkirk and Galashiels had to admit, albeit reluctantly, that Hawick was the epicentre of this flourishing industry and, during its days of glory, in some ways separated from the rest of Scottish Borders life. Even the accent in Hawick was different, coloured, some say, by incomers from Edinburgh, Glasgow and, though few locals care to admit this, from as far afield as the dark dales of Yorkshire, south of a wall built by Emperor Hadrian to protect the inhabitants of Scotland from invaders. Well, this would have been the view of the Celts dwelling in the Teviot **Valley** back then.*

Professor Peregrine Pringle, however, spoke differently. His was an educated Edinburgh Morningside accent. The small, sprightly man, whose tousled black hair resembled a chambermaid's mop, worked in the University of Edinburgh. Exactly what he did up there, a half-day's horse ride away, remained a mystery, but the man's genius had become local legend. As had his house, Number Twenty-four.

A large stone mansion at the end of a long lane, it had always been known as Number Twenty-four. The professor lived alone. Despite the size of the building, there were no servants. Why Number 'Twenty-four', when it stood by itself, no one knew. Most of the week it was empty, for the professor took a horse-drawn carriage to Edinburgh every Monday morning to do whatever he did in that European centre of learning—the 'Athens of the North'—only to return on Saturday afternoon. This went on for years until one April, following the coldest, bleakest winter within living memory.

A thick blanket of snow had carpeted the Scottish Borders since the week before Christmas, and no one saw the little professor for almost four months. Number Twenty-four, with its shuttered-up windows, seemed, like a grizzly bear, to have lapsed into seasonal slumber, the only sign of life being the large black crows nesting in its sole companion in those days: a spreading yew tree that had become heavy with snow. Even the crows remained silent that winter.

The professor returned in the spring, with the thaw, and he no longer travelled up to Edinburgh during the week. All night long, a light would remain on in one of the upstairs rooms.

"Aye, he must be working on something really important," folk would gossip. "Like he's aboot to change the world or something." Others were less complimentary: "Got kicked oot o' the University," one woman said. "Too friendly wi' the Dean's wife," was another suggestion.

Professor Pringle was unmarried. At first this was easily explained in Hawick:

"He's far too clever, ken. No woman could put up wi' a

brain like that!"

But this made no sense, for one thing was certain. He was incredibly wealthy. Which is why no one questioned the rumour that had spread throughout the town by the end of April: that the professor was planning a trip to South America. The only thing about which they did argue was the reason for this trip.

Few believed the initial explanation: that he was going to seek out a wife because no right-minded Scots lass would be silly enough to marry a man with hair like that and who cooked for himself. More likely seemed a later rumour: that this was to be a journey of exploration to make the greatest discovery of not only the nineteenth century but of all time. The professor was, folk whispered in Hawick, about to uncover the mystery of life. In South America.

He was away for four months, returning in a big, black coach in the autumn when the trees were dappled red, orange and yellow. Whatever had been in that coach was, someone said, quickly transferred to the coal house in the back garden of Number Twenty-four.

The coal house was unusually large for the purpose suggested by its title, but it had no windows, which is why everyone called it a coal house. Passers-by (or rather, locals who went up the lane to spy on the professor and to be first with the latest news about him) said the door was always open. Also, strange, other-worldly noises emerged from the outbuilding.

Then, one day, when the leaves had turned brown and were beginning to decorate the lane leading up to Number Twenty-four, word spread around the marketplace, and in the bars, that the professor was gone.

"Gone? Cannae be! We'd have seen the carriage if he was off on his travels," was the standard reply to the latest news.

But he was never seen again whilst Queen Victoria sat on her throne. Nor through the reigns of two Edwards and two Georges. The land around Number Twenty-four was bought by a developer, streets appeared, and a housing estate grew up around the house which no builder dared demolish. When development plans were drawn up, houses were numbered so that the small two-storey home to the left of the professor's house was Number Twenty-three, and that to right of it, Number Twenty-five.

When the professor returned towards the end of the twentieth century, his mop of hair had turned white. Apart from this, he was still sprightly, and, as before, he travelled up to Edinburgh University, returning to Hawick at weekends when the door to the coal house would remain open day and night, as it had been a hundred years ago. Once again, eerie, humming sounds were heard.

Then there were the disappearances and, according to local children, mysterious transformations. Ducks were mentioned.

"What nonsense oor bairns fill their wee heads with," parents would say in the supermarkets and the bars. Those bairns grew up and, in the twenty-first century, they said the same thing about their children. And these children would giggle, then quack like ducks...

Chapter 1

"Just shut him up or I'll wring his scrawny neck!"

That's blown it, thought Dylan as his dad stepped back from the open window and limped out of the bedroom. Things had grown tense between them after the man said no way would he pay for Dylan to waste his life helping furry creatures that go around leaving their poop all over the pavements. Now it was open warfare. Before this angry outburst, the lad reckoned he might have stood a chance with Alice Chang if she knew that, one day, he was going to be a vet. Now the slim neck of that chance that had been wrung rather than Bouncer's.

The boy hid behind a curtain so as not to be seen whilst he peered down to survey the damage. Alice stood open-mouthed on the lawn next door, staring up at his bedroom window. Bouncer sat beside her with his tongue lolling and his head cocked sideways. Dylan cursed his father. How could he ever get to talk to the girl now?

Alice Chang's father ran the local Chinese restaurant in Hawick High Street. Or rather, her family, Alice included, did. Most evenings and weekends, she helped out by serving customers, which made her hugely popular at school for she'd often sneak her classmates extra bags of prawn crackers whilst her dad wasn't looking. When not in the Happy Palace she was usually in her back garden with Bouncer, or taking him for a walk. Dylan had reassured his dad that she always had one of those polythene bags with her, so Bouncer never left his poop behind in the street, but Mr Ross said his germs would still be there on the pavement and that Alice's dog, like all other canines, was a threat to mankind.

Dylan's dad being their maths teacher at the high school did not help. Nor did the fact that Dylan always came top in most subjects however much he tried not to. Alice was hopeless at maths. Dylan had recently fantasised about giving her private maths lessons. Now those fantasies had been flung out of the window by his father's fit of rage.

Curse Dad and his limp! Alice, too, might now join in the fun next time Colin McPhail mimics that limp in front of me. "Watch out for him, girls! Might be catching," the wise-cracker teased the other day. "In his genes. Jeans— genes! Get it?"

Dylan dreaded school the following Monday. Not only would she ignore him, but he'd never get the chance to say 'ni hao'. He had been practising Chinese for 'hello' every morning in the shower. Got it off the internet. It was the next step in his strategy. If his Chinese impressed Alice, perhaps she'd allow him to coach her in mathematics.

Who knows what this might lead to?

He had even day-dreamt the impossible: sitting next to her, their elbows touching, whilst he tried to make algebra simple for his pretty classmate.

As predicted, Monday was a total nightmare. The Chinese girl refused to look at him. That was bad enough, but to see her chatting away to that pimply, red-faced rugby buff, Colin, during lunch break, was like the end of the world. Tuesday was worse. She sat next to Colin at lunch. In the evening, Dylan nearly panicked when he saw a guy with Colin-sized muscles, and a dog, creep past his front gate towards the Changs' place wearing a brown tunic and sandals. Thankfully he had brown hair, not black like Colin's. The face was wrong, too. Designer-stubble wasn't

Colin's image. Not yet.

That was another thing. Dylan had recently started to use a razor every day, even though he had nothing to shave, whereas Colin's square jaw was already like that of a man. Dylan forever hoped to see that jaw appear in class one morning with a sticking plaster covering a sliced-off pimple.

After the mysterious figure in a tunic passed by the Changs' house, Dylan felt he could breathe again. Maybe, he wondered, the guy was a walk-on for a low-budget movie about the battling Borders Reivers of the past. *But why the dog?* He thought little more about it, particularly after his life hit rock bottom the following day.

Colin walked Alice **home. Not** only that, but he went inside her house and later, from his bedroom window, Dylan saw the Chinese girl and Colin cavorting together in her back garden. Bouncer was licking his rival's hand. That did it! War on two fronts. With his dad about becoming a vet and with Colin over Alice. Trouble was, Colin trained in a gym most evenings, and it showed in his muscles. What if Alice were to watch him play rugby that coming Saturday? She'd see those accursed muscles in action. Something had to be done before then.

Sadly, Dylan's head remained empty of a solution until Friday night when he glimpsed a notice sellotaped to a lamppost—one against which he'd once seen Bouncer lift a leg. Bouncer now sat displayed on the notice, with his tongue, as usual, hanging out. Above his photo, Dylan read the word 'REWARD'. It didn't say what the reward would be. Perhaps, the boy wondered, **a sackful** of prawn crackers, although, in truth, he would accept just a 'hello' from Alice. If offered.

So... Bouncer's missing!

In a flash, Dylan saw an acceptable future. He would find Bouncer. Not only might Alice then allow him to say 'hello' in Mandarin, and give her private maths coaching, but he pictured a new suitor, Dylan Ross, replacing his rival in her garden and having both hands licked by Bouncer. In fact, he might even let the dog lick his face. Good practice for being a vet, he reckoned, and bound to impress the girl.

It was already getting dark when he finished his supper. He informed his parents that he was going outside to get some exercise to "build up my muscles". His annoying young sister, Caitlin, said that could never happen because he didn't have any to build up. She suggested he go to the nearby Lidl store, instead, to buy some, so he slammed the front door, as loudly as possible, on his way out, and vowed not to return until he had found Alice's dog.

***

The previous day, Bouncer lay curled up, like a canine croissant, on the kitchen floor. A bold knock on the back door made his ears flick up. He stood, wagging his tail, expecting his human mistress to enter and give him a bone or something to play with. How he adored that girl! When she vanished during the day, life became a total bore, but there were those wonderful two days out of every seven (he was good at maths—for a dog) when she would take him down to the park across the river from Wilton Lodge for a taste of freedom. Or let him run around in the garden at the back of the house. If only she could bark, or he could speak, he had often dreamt, things would be a lot more fun, for there was so much they could tell each other.

It wasn't his mistress. It was an odd-looking, unshaven human with shaggy hair resembling that of an unkempt spaniel he'd once seen in the park. Plus, it barked. *And* it wore a brown dress. Not one of those colourful pretty ones Alice sometimes wore, but more of a sack like the plastic bags his mistress would take out to the rubbish bin. Never had he seen a male human dressed in such a way. And why was it there? Had it come to teach Alice how to bark?

Behind the human stood a squat Scottie wagging his tail, with his head held at an inquisitive angle. He, too, barked, but the barks made no sense. Like when humans 'woofed' at him. Then the human barked. Bouncer understood. This was nothing to do with teaching Alice. He was to follow them out of the house. *'Alice must allow you to go,'* barked the human. *'For the sake of all dogkind.'*

***

Being good at maths meant that Dylan was methodical. He reckoned a vet had to be methodical if he or she wished to successfully cure sick animals. He decided to tackle this search for Bouncer in a scientific way. First, he should look for poops. Dad was right. Dogs do crap almost anywhere. Without Alice and her polythene bag, Bouncer would be unable to conceal the evidence. It wouldn't only be bugs left behind on the pavement. So, armed with a torch, Dylan set off up the street on one side of the road, back, in parallel, along the other, then, turning the corner, did the same thing in the next street—and the next and the next.

For a maths-dumb, sports-enthusiast like Colin, this would have been an onerous chore, but the complicated exercise made Dylan perfectly happy. He could think of no better way to spend a Friday night than to search for the poop of Alice's missing pet in the streets of Hawick. Plus, it gave him an opportunity to multi-task. In his head, whilst scanning the pavement, he practised saying not only *'ni hao'*, but also *'xie xie'*, Chinese for 'thank you'. He had discovered, on the internet, it's pronounced 'sheer sheer', and reckoned that when he'd found and returned the adventurous dog to its rightful owner, he would be able to understand the girl if she were to thank him in Chinese. Sheer heaven!

Alice was always talking to her parents in Chinese whenever he went to collect a takeaway from the Happy Palace. After his father's appalling behaviour the previous weekend, not only did he *not* receive an extra bag of prawn crackers on Thursday night, but the girl didn't even smile. In fact, she scowled. Things had to change, and before Alice watched Colin play rugby at the weekend. Dylan felt sure that Colin, who came bottom in most subjects other than rugby, and whose brain would have easily fitted into a pencil sharpener, would never be able to multi-task. And not in a month of Sundays could that dimwit say 'ni hao' like a Chinese person. So, Bouncer had to be found.

If only I could slow down time, thought Dylan after an hour had gone by and all he'd discovered was one shrivelled, sausage-shaped dog poop in a gutter the other side of Hawick. *At least it's in the gutter!* It was almost black, and Dylan felt certain Bouncer, being a young goldador, would produce a lighter-coloured excrement, perhaps with a yellowish tinge. Whatever, there was no sign of Bouncer and his confidence fizzled like a dying firework. He was about to give up and return home (*tail between my legs*, he mused, tragically) when a squat, white Scottie appeared from nowhere and bounded up to him.

***

The Scottie spoke in human-talk to the stubbled man who bent down and barked a single word into Bouncer's ear. The word was electrifying. Bouncer jumped up at the human

10

stranger and licked whatever he could reach. *If only humans weren't so tall!* The Scottie chuckled just like the boy Alice lived with. A boy whose facial resemblance to Alice suggested they were from the same litter.

Bouncer trotted along behind the Scottie whilst the human barked at him about being needed somewhere special. It sounded exciting. *'Bones galore to chew on,'* the human promised. But when they stopped outside the gate of the grim, grey house that Alice always hurried past, Bouncer wanted to turn back. *'I don't like this place,'* he barked. *'And where's Alice?'*

Bouncer hated being without his owner. It was as if half of him **were** missing. Their human/dog friendship made him feel more complete when they were together, although he was fully aware that most humans went around without dogs. Incomplete humans, as far as he was concerned. But here he was, being dog-barked at by a strange human, and being told to enter that unfriendly building where *'everything will be different'*. If this meant being without Alice, he didn't fancy 'different'. Until…

***

Dylan bent down and patted the eager little animal.

"Yes, tragic!" he said as he tickled the dog under the chin. "Have you by any chance got a girlfriend dog? Or perhaps…?" He glanced underneath the Scottie, but there was too much fur for him to tell. "Maybe you're a girl anyway. In which case, you might be able to help me. Female intuition, it's called. How can I ever impress Alice if I can't get Bouncer back for her? And I'm not even interested in the reward, ken. That's neither here nor there as far as I'm concerned."

Dylan had the distinct impression that the dog frowned

when he said this. Whatever, there was something strange about the animal. The tilt of its head, perhaps? Its eyes? Its nose and the way it seemed to sniff the air? Was it sniffing for Bouncer? Trying to help Dylan in his terrible plight?

One thing seemed certain. This dog understood. Understood what Dylan was trying to say and understood his dilemma: that Bouncer had to be found before Alice got to see Colin's muscles on the rugby pitch. So, when the Scottie took off, periodically stopping and looking back to check that Dylan was still there, the boy followed. All the way back to the street around the corner from his and Alice's two-storey houses. Wagging its stumpy tail, it halted outside the three-storey Number Twenty-four and waited for him to catch up.

There was only one thing in the world that Dylan would not do for Alice: enter the garden of Number Twenty-four. Everyone knew about Number Twenty-four, though few talked in public about the place, let alone its mysterious, batty owner, Professor Peregrine Pringle. Rumours about the eccentric old man were so ingrained in local folklore that nobody knew exactly who had said what about him, and no one in Hawick had any idea what he was a professor of. Some said he came from Glasgow, others suggested that Peregrine sounded English. 'Romanian with a name change' was also offered. Mostly, the man was simply referred to as 'Him' when talked about, and no person in their right mind would stop outside Number Twenty-four as this Scottie dog had done.

***

"A bitch?" queried Bouncer, barking back at the human in their shared language.

"A beautiful bitch called Bosona," affirmed the human

in its curious, but understandable, dog-speak—a limited language at the best of times. The Scottie blinked and made a whimpering sound for Bouncer's benefit, an attempt to express the beauty of the bitch in question. She was being held captive, but this was about all he could get from the human. He learned more from the tail wags and head tilts of the Scottie. It seemed she could be his if he were to win the bitch's heart by rescuing her. But what about Alice?

The human failed to understand Bouncer's dilemma, unlike the Scottie who told his shabby owner to reach down and remove Bouncer's red collar. On instructions from his dog, the man dropped this onto the path before opening the front door of the house of which Bouncer's human owner had always been so fearful. Against his better judgement, and lured by visions of a beautiful bitch, the **goldador** followed the Scottie into the house, wagging his tail.

***

As the Scottie looked up, its head at a questioning angle, Dylan's own head did battle with his legs. They remained rooted to the ground whilst his brain tried to persuade them to at least deliver him to where the Scottie stood, wagging its tail, at the gate of Number Twenty-four. It wasn't as if he'd be going inside the house.

"No harm in that," he said out loud to his legs. "We'll stay together on the pavement. Might be my only chance with Alice. Tomorrow there's a rugby match. Afterwards it'll be too late. She'll be swooning over Mr Muscleman. So... move, you mindless limbs!"

The Scottie woofed at him. It now wagged its tail so furiously that Dylan feared the little appendage might drop off. The boy's legs finally conceded and, slowly, walked him towards the dog. After all, there was no hard evidence that he would get turned into a duck as kids in P1 used to say. For all anyone knew, Professor Pringle could be a brilliant scientist about to save the world from some terrifying catastrophe. Indeed, if he, Dylan Ross, were to assist in this process, he might get more than a 'hello' from Alice. Or perhaps the professor had a secret formula for growing muscles bigger than those of Colin McPhail.

The Scottie jumped up at Dylan, resting its paws on the boy's knees. It barked again, an odd-sounding bark, got down, spun around in giddying circles then jumped up again. Dylan dropped to his heels to pet and pat the dog. Then he looked up at Number Twenty-four.

The lights in the house were off, the curtains closed. One of the windows had a diagonal crack outlined with brown sticky tape. The front garden was overgrown with weeds and had no flowers, but there was something red on the path near the front door. Bouncer had a red collar. The gate was open. Dylan stood up. Whilst he argued again with his legs whether, or not, to cross the threshold into the garden, the Scottie waddled off up the path, picked up the red object in his jaws and returned with it. After dropping the collar at Dylan's feet, the dog barked and barked—but there was something odd about the barks. Like a human going 'woof, woof'.

Dylan reached down and turned over the collar to read 'BOUNCER', with a telephone number, engraved in red, on a brass disc.

"Thanks, buddy! Good boy!"

Happier than he'd felt for many years, he stroked the dog. Then, holding what was surely the most precious object in the multiverse, he turned to leave. He had only gone a few paces when...

"You're welcome!"

Dylan froze. He half-turned. The Scottie stood, still wagging its tail, looking up at him. Dylan's gaze travelled to take in the house, the garden, the rest of the street, including the rooftops, but there was no one around. He shrugged his shoulders.

Funny the things you hear when a whole load's been taken off your mind, he thought.

***

Bouncer sniffed a blend of dog smells every bit as powerful as what he had once experienced at the annual Kelso dog show. Was he about to meet this beautiful bitch? Would there be rivals around? He had seen dogs fight in the park, but biting anything other than food, or a bone, wasn't his thing. He followed the Scottie into a room full of dogs of all shapes and sizes, including bitches, although there were none that could be described as beautiful. Some dogs yapped, some talked, like Scottie, whilst others lapped at a yellowish liquid from huge dog bowls. Bouncer stood watching. Dogs that yapped turned into speaking dogs after drinking from these bowls. Scottie's cocked head informed Bouncer that he, too, should drink.

Never had he tasted anything so delicious. Although not particularly thirsty, he simply had to drink and drink. Something strange started to happen in his throat, as if a whole new world was opening up there. This feeling spread throughout his body. Things became clearer. Alice was his pet, not the other way around. And when he could drink no more, he looked up and burped.

"Feeling better?" asked Scottie.

"Feeling great!" replied Bouncer. "So—where's the bitch?"

***

Dylan headed for home but got no further than the street corner. Something tugged at his trouser leg. He looked down. It was the white Scottie. Although the dog had quite possibly saved him from a life of Alice-less misery, or at least given him an excuse to talk to the girl (his brain was still trying to work out what to say to her), the little animal was beginning to annoy him. A bit like **his sister** used to when he didn't want to play with her. Now Caitlin had given up on him entirely and they only communicated if one wished to irritate the other.

"Good doggie, but you can go back home now. I said, 'Thank you!'"

"But you didn't say how the collar on its own will help."

Dylan almost dropped the object. It was definitely the dog who had spoken. For a few moments, he stood as if his brain had been emptied of all reason.

A talking dog? Only happens in the movies. And certainly not **here** *in Hawick.*

"I mean, what's she gonna do with just a collar?"

That canine creature down there really did speak. I saw its mouth move as the words came out. And they made sense. They shouldn't, should they? Words shouldn't come out of a dog. If they do, they shouldn't make any sense.

"A boy," announced the Scottie for Dylan's information.

"What?"

"Me. I'm a boy. You said back there, 'maybe you're a girl'. I'm not. I'm a boy dog. I'll show you." The Scottie raised a hind leg, but Dylan looked away.

"Okay! I believe you. But how come you speak?"

"You mean, how come *you* speak? In my dimension, humans only woof. It's all so weird here. I've sort of got used

16

to it, though. Thinking of getting my pet human to speak, too. Hope it'll sound better than my woofs."

"Why didn't you speak straightaway?"

"Afraid you'd run off like a scaredy-cat."

"Alice watching Colin play rugby is the only thing that scares me!"

"Uh?"

"Okay, so you can talk. Where's Bouncer? I've gotta get him back. Because of *her*. Before that rugby match tomorrow."

"Bouncer never mentioned he played anything called rugby. Hey, son—what's up?" Dylan felt the dog's eyes bore into his sadness.

"Not Bouncer, stupid! This is all about Alice. Bouncer's her dog, see. And there's a serious risk that an idiot called Colin will become her boyfriend. The **dude's** a rugby buff. Muscles like Godzilla!"

"Oh, it's all so strange here in Hawick. Can't get used to it. This Alice person is Bouncer's human pet, then. He said something about a young human bitch. **Or 'girl', as you lot would say.**"

"Pet? If you must put it that way round, yes. Sort of. So, where is he? Where's Bouncer?"

The Scottie glanced at Number Twenty-four. "Why should I tell you?"

Dylan's brain did a mental somersault as it tried to think of an answer. "Because of Alice," he replied. "She'll be missing him."

"That's not a good answer. Suppose he's not missing her." Dylan could not imagine anyone, person or dog, not missing the Chinese girl.

"Oh, he will be," he assured the dog.

"Why?"

"Because—" Dylan felt himself blush.

"You've changed colour," observed the Scottie. "Spit it out."

"Because she's pretty. Prettier than all the other girls at school put together."

"Why would you want to put a whole bunch of girls together? Don't they make enough noise barking on their own?"

"Figure of speech. Anyway, girls in Hawick don't bark. Not the ones I know. Look, Alice is both pretty and kind to animals. Bouncer *must* love her. All males do. Plus, she gives Bouncer bones to chew on. Sometimes prawn crackers, ken."

"Prawn crackers? Hmm! Be back outside Number Twenty-four at the crack of dawn. Before he returns."

"He?"

"The professor. Once he's back, and the sun's up, they'll all be gone."

"Can you promise Bouncer will be there?" asked Dylan. The last thing he wanted to do was to raise Alice's hopes only to let her down.

"If you bring enough prawn crackers."

"I'll ask Alice."

The dog gave a grunt and scampered up the path to Number Twenty-four. To the house where the boy was once convinced that he'd get turned into a duck should he ever be fool enough to enter it. Perhaps, he wondered, the Scottie had previously been a human then, via duck, and because of Number Twenty-four, got transformed into dog.

Grinning like a Cheshire cat, Dylan approached the Changs' house, dog collar in hand. If confidence were like a tree, his would now be the size of a Californian Redwood, the largest free-standing member of the vegetable kingdom in the world. He even felt pity for rugby-playing Colin as his finger touched the doorbell button. This produced a little tune which made him want to sing out. Alice could have her first exciting maths lesson the following morning rather than stand around watching a load of pimpled boys chase each other in the mud (it usually rained in Hawick at the weekend).

The door opened. Dylan's heart stumbled. It was Alice's big brother, Ben...

Goddamnit!

Chapter 2

Bouncer learned a lot from Scottie. The little dog took him to one side and said how he would soon become a master in his own right in a land where humans were pets and dogs ruled. The bitch in question, the beautiful Bosona, was, like himself, a golden Labrador retriever, or 'goldador', and the true Top Dog, only she was languishing in her own dungeon, threatened with the Bitch Ditch by a cruel tyrant of a rottweiler, Bruiser, whose forces had wiped out those of the great General Scratch.

"The Bitch Ditch?" queried Bouncer.

"You don't want to know!" answered Scottie. "Just join BUDS. Bosona's United Dog Squad. Become a 'buddy'. Help to free Bosona and she might even choose you. As her partner, that is."

Bouncer wagged his tail with excitement. A female dog at long last! He did love Alice, but this was so different. A bitch to call a mate would transform his life. He wanted to bark about it, but only words emerged from his mouth:

"Hey, man, a goldador bitch! That is so cool!"

***

"Yes?" queried Ben.

Dylan struggled to find the right words. His brain hadn't planned for Ben. He raised the collar up for Ben to see.

"Um... Alice," he said meekly.

"What about Alice? She doesn't usually wear one of those." Ben pointed to the collar. "Perhaps she should, though." The Chinese boy grinned broadly. "Might be able to keep track of her, then!" Ben had a mischievous twinkle in his eyes that totally upended Dylan's confidence. The redwood became a droopy two-leafed sapling. Ben winked. "All these boys now, see!"

All these boys? The sapling shrank to a single-celled diatom.

"No—I mean her what-do-you-call-it. Golden thingummy. Labrador. Her lost dog, like. Bouncer. The Scottie says—that is, the talking dog—"

"Alice!"

"What?"

Oh, my God... her voice! What the heck—?

"One of your boyfriends. I think he's having a spot of bother explaining himself here. Something to do with Bouncer."

"I haven't got any boyfriends, Not yet! And what d'you mean 'to do with Bouncer'?"

Dylan heard someone come down the stairs. Close to panic, the thought of turning and running away bounced like a tennis ball between the redwood and the diatom: redwood stay, diatom run. He thought of Alice and Colin in the garden together and, spurred on by anger, the redwood won.

Ben was replaced by Alice at the front door. Dylan wanted to say '*Ni hao!*' but no words, Chinese or otherwise, came out. He held up the red dog collar, as he'd done for Ben, but said nothing. The girl snatched the collar from him.

"It's you!" Alice exclaimed, her disappointment painfully obvious. "How did you get hold of this?" she asked. She examined it carefully as if to make sure it hadn't been damaged by Dylan. The Chinese girl then looked scornfully up at her neighbour who remained glued to the doorstep like a shop-fitter's dummy. Her eyes, as delicious as ever, had become distinctly dangerous. In fact, it seemed she was about to explode.

"I—um—this Scottie dog, see—" Dylan fought against his shyness as he attempted to tell her how he came upon the dog collar.

"Bouncer's a goldador, not a Scottie. What are you talking about?"

"Number Twenty-four. The professor's house around the corner. There's a talking dog—"

"*That* place? Are you completely mad?"

"No. He says that if—"

"It's Mr. Ross, isn't it? That horrid father of yours!" Tears appeared in the corners of Alice's eyes. The very last thing he wanted to do was to make the girl cry.

"No, please. It's nothing to do with my—"

Clutching the red collar to her chest, Alice burst into tears.

"Your father's killed Bouncer and hidden his body there! I hate him! I hate *you*! Go away! I never want to see you again. I'll ask my parents if I can go to Selkirk High School instead, so I won't have to. Or even go to stay with my aunt in China!" Each statement, sounding worse than the previous one, caused Dylan to break out into a cold sweat.

"Alice, please! Listen to—"

Bang! The door slammed in his face.

It was a long drop from that top-of-the-world feeling to the depths of despair, but that's the journey young Dylan Ross was forced to take as he stared at the Changs' closed front door.

Like the collar, it was red. He'd learned from his dad, after the man had been to Hong Kong, that red is a lucky colour for the Chinese. This knowledge inspired his next and only possible course of action…

***

Bouncer was taken to a back-garden bustling with talking dogs. Most were from Hawick, although some came from further afield. A few lived in Galashiels, a couple were from Kelso whilst a rather confused dachshund had no idea where he was from. A "tiny cottage with an old lady who always wears brown, the same colour as me," was all he could come up with.

Talk centred around 'passing over'. Apparently, this involved going into a building at the back (called a coal house) where the 'Vortex' would transport all talking dogs to Dogtopia. There they were to become soldiers.

"You mean we fight? Like those ugly dogs in the park Alice takes me to?" Bouncer sounded unhappy.

"Oh, park dogs aren't *real* fighters!" the dachshund assured him. "In Dogtopia it's to the death."

Bouncer hesitated. Did he really have to go into that building? After all, he loved Alice and loved his life with her. Having no inclination for fighting, he favoured an easy existence. There again, a beautiful goldador bitch for real—not just in his dreams…?

With head held high, Bouncer walked on into the coal house.

***

It was getting late, but rather than deterring Dylan, this urged him on. Always top in English, writing came naturally to the boy. Far more easily than speaking. Choosing a red pen, for Chinese reasons, he began his letter:

My Dear Alice,

He halted, looked at what he'd written then screwed up the sheet. *Not yet, dumbo!* Taking a fresh sheet of A4 paper (from the bottom of the ream to make sure it wasn't in any conceivable way damaged) he began again...

Dear Alice Chang,
I think I know where Bouncer is. I hate my dad as much as you do because I want to be a vet one day and he says he won't let me but, honestly, he knows nothing about me. Or Bouncer. I found your pet's collar in front of Number Twenty-four and a dog said...

Dylan stopped, re-read what he'd written, crossed out 'a dog' then continued...

...someone said to get Bouncer back you must be at the professor's house before dawn tomorrow. I looked that up on the internet and it'll be at 5 o'clock in the morning. I do hope that's not too early for you. If you don't make it, they said you might never see Bouncer again.

The last sentence was, Dylan reckoned, a necessary embellishment. His dad had told him about the Chinese triads being like the Mafia, and this little twist in the truth had a hint of Mafia threat about it. She would perhaps admire a guy who had the guts to stand up to the mob more than a lump of muscle who enjoyed chasing Jedburgh around the rugby pitch.

I'll be there to help if you want me to, but if you tell me to go away again I will.

Yours <u>very</u> sincerely,

Dylan Ross

Dylan re-read the letter several times and saw nothing in it that might make her cross again. He hoped. He wanted to close with 'XXX' but feared this would be taken the wrong way. He did, however, add a PS:

Please bring some sort of a weapon. We might need it if we meet the professor. I think we should each have one. Plus, please bring a bag of prawn crackers.

The sapling had grown to the size of a small Christmas tree. Large enough for the boy to carefully fold the letter and slip it into an envelope on which he wrote:

Absolutely private. Only for Miss Alice Chang.

He sat on his bed for a while, passing the letter from one hand to the other, until he could summon enough courage to go next door again. Thirteen-year-old Caitlin, in her pyjamas, stood on the landing and watched him creep downstairs to the front door.

"You're being very mysterious tonight, big brother!" she said.

"Shhh! I'll give you some money for sweets tomorrow if you keep your mouth shut," Dylan replied.

"You won't! I know you!"

He was about to say he was deadly serious this time, but she quickly disappeared back into her room. Next door, Ben answered again. Dylan was relieved. He didn't think he could handle any more tears from the girl he so wished to befriend.

"Please just give this to Alice," he said to Ben, handing the older boy his letter.

"Oooh! Big mystery, ay?"

"Please do it. Tell her it's for Bouncer's sake, not mine."

Ben nodded and smiled. Dylan liked him. He was an irrepressibly cheerful soul, and, seeing the Chang family in action at the Happy Palace, he got the impression that Alice was extremely fond of her big brother.

"Okay," Ben agreed, winking at Dylan. Dylan winked back, although he didn't know why.

The boy set his alarm for 4.30am. Enough time, he reckoned, for a quick snack and shower. He could hardly call this a date, but a shower to render him totally smell-free seemed essential. Perhaps it would reduce the risk of Alice attacking him with her weapon, should she bring one, because of his smell. Between 4.50am and 5 o'clock, he stood in the dim light of early dawn, outside the Changs' front gate, holding a ridiculous Superman rucksack (his dad refused to buy him a new one) which contained a small packet of Sugar Puffs, the next best thing to prawn crackers, he reckoned, and his 'weapon'. When her face appeared at an upstairs window, his mind began to dance the Highland Fling.

What shall I say, what shall I say... what the heck can I say? Dylan asked himself over and over. When the Changs' front door opened, and she appeared, impossibly lovely in tight jeans and a blue sweater, and carrying something in her hand, he began to mouth the words:

Ni hao, ni hao, ni hao...

"Hello," Alice said.

"Oh—hi! Thanks. I mean... thanks for coming."

"Ben told me to say 'sorry'. For being rude last night. Do you forgive me?" Dylan had no idea what to say. All he could do was nod like a puppet. "Look, you were trying to tell me something about Bouncer and I sent you away, right?" she added.

"Yes—I mean no. I didn't explain myself very well. Not good with speaking words. My fault."

"No, it wasn't. I was just upset about Bouncer. Will this do?" The girl held out a pair of dressmaking scissors. "They're Mummy's. All I could think of for a weapon. I'm not into fighting."

Dylan was about to say he wasn't either, but then thought that might make him sound weak compared with muscleman Colin.

"Perfect. I've got—um—this. It's mine, like!" he said proudly, opening his rucksack, with Superman facing away from the girl, before extracting the small penknife he'd bought in Edinburgh. It had a picture of the Scott Monument on it and he hoped she would be impressed. She wasn't.

"Did you bring the prawn crackers?"

"No! They're only for my friends."

A hint well taken!

"Oh. Well, um... we'd better hurry," the boy suggested, feeling well and truly deflated. Together they headed around the corner for Number Twenty-four.

"So, who is it who told you I must go there to find Bouncer this morning?" Alice asked. "I really didn't take in what you said last night." Dylan was afraid she would just run back home if he were to tell her the truth.

"Wasn't a girl," he replied. He hated lying, so decided to say as little as possible.

"You said something about having to get there before the professor comes back. You don't really believe that business about him turning people into ducks, do you? My brother says it's total nonsense."

"It wasn't a duck that said it either," Dylan answered truthfully. "That's for sure."

"Why did you call me Alice Chang in your letter and not just Alice?" she asked.

"Thought there was a better chance you'd read it if I stayed formal."

"Formal? You *are* angry with me, aren't you? I said sorry!"

Dylan felt things were beginning to slip towards the dangerous territory of 'cross girl'. Having a younger sister, he knew that territory only too well.

"Not at all angry, I promise. Just didn't want to hurt your feelings. And—um—respect. I thought Alice Chang sounded more respectful."

"Oh!"

"Anyway, I like Chinese names. Like Chang. I can say '*ni hao*', you know."

Alice giggled.

"Not like that! It's *ni hao*. Your tones are wrong."

Tones? Wrong?

"Thank you," Dylan said. He so wanted to suggest that she teach him Chinese in exchange for maths lessons, but they had already arrived at Number Twenty-four. He opened out his penknife.

"Better be prepared," he warned. "Hold your scissors up. Like this!" He raised her hand and opened out the scissors for her. The girl's hand felt pleasantly soft and warm. Normally he'd be in bed at this hour. How would her hand feel in bed? He blushed at the thought of this.

"What are you doing with those scissors and that penknife?"

Dylan recognised the voice. Unlike Alice, he wasn't surprised it came from the ground near Alice's feet, but the girl dropped the scissors from shock. Dylan picked them up. Alice, with her mouth agape, pointed at the Scottie.

"You said she's the prettiest in your school. I was hoping for a poodle or something special, but—just another human, ay?"

Alice, still staring with wide eyes at the talking dog, grabbed Dylan's arm.

"My turn to apologise," he told his neighbour, "but I honestly didn't think you'd believe me. Sorry. I should've explained better."

"Dogs don't talk," was all she could say. "Not even Bouncer talks."

"He will where he's going," said Scottie.

"Where's that?" asked Dylan.

Afraid that Alice might faint or something (he'd read about girls fainting), he tried to support her, penknife in one hand. She moved away from him.

"Where I come from. And the professor. Our dimension," explained Scottie.

"Where's Bouncer?" asked Dylan. He felt annoyed that Alice's pet wasn't there.

"Inside."

"The—um—the house? In *there*?"

"He'll be in the coal house. At the back."

"Is it safe? I do feel responsible for Alice, you know."

"Safer than out here. You don't want Scissorman to find you, do you?"

"You mean the professor?"

"What are you talking about?"

"How do we get in, then?"

The dog saw Dylan glance at a window criss-crossed with sticky tape.

"Easiest way is to use the door. I don't think he'd be too happy if you broke another one of his windows. It was a pit bull did that. Vicious brutes, they are."

"I know a guy with a friendly pit bull," someone behind Dylan said. The boy swivelled, expecting another taking dog. He was both dismayed and relieved to see Ben standing there. Dismayed because any chance of impressing Alice in the presence of her beloved big brother was hugely diminished, but relieved because he had a strange feeling that they were going to need a guy like Ben. Alice ran to her brother and hugged him.

If only I could be Ben just for a few blissful moments!

Beside Ben stood Dylan's sister. His brain tried to persuade his eyes they were just seeing things, but it was painfully true. Worst of all, she was wearing the short red dress that she had on for her birthday party nearly a year ago, before she began to fill out, plus her red shoes with raised heels. Already, she looked fifteen.

"What on earth are you doing here, Caitlin?"

"I had to see what was going on. You were acting so odd last night. And I heard you get up early. Looked out the window and saw Ben follow you and Alice."

"You'd better watch out, Ben," Dylan warned. "Caitlin's in love with you!"

"I can easily cure that. With a bowl of Chinese noodles," chuckled Ben.

"What?" queried Caitlin. She looked alarmed. A threat that Ben might tip noodles over her head, perhaps?

Alice laughed. "You should see my brother slurp his noodles with chopsticks!" she explained. "It's gross! Like his mouth turns into a vacuum cleaner."

"Will you teach me to do that, Ben?" Caitlin asked.

Dylan couldn't help thinking that in a few years' time his sister would be quite a stunner, with her beautiful blue eyes and wavy red hair, so long as she kept her mouth shut.

"I've got red underwear on too!" she proudly announced. "Maybe you'd like to see my red—?"

"That's enough, Caitlin!"

Dylan's sister pouted.

"Thank the Great Dog humans only woof where I come from," said Scottie. "Now, do you want to see Bouncer again or not?"

"Oh *please!*" begged Alice, breaking free from her brother. "I want him home. He's my best friend ever!"

"Yes, he did say he wanted to say goodbye to someone called Alice before leaving. Guess that's you, right?"

"Leaving? But where to?"

Dylan was afraid Alice might start to cry again. Thankfully he'd come prepared. There was a handkerchief in his pocket.

"Let him explain himself. He's somewhere on the other side of that door."

Alice glanced at Dylan. The boy's big chance. He, not elder brother Ben, was the chosen one. The one she turned to when the chips were down. The one who might lead her into the unknown. His confidence swelled to oak tree size as he swaggered up the path towards the front door of Number Twenty-four, watched by the others.

It was already a fraction open. All that was needed was a little nudge. He glanced back at Caitlin and their Chinese neighbours standing on the other side of the gate. Alice's gorgeous eyes were still trained on him and he tried to imagine he was her favourite actor in a Hollywood movie, the good guy with muckle muscles who was about take on a giant of a bad guy. Something of a cross between Darth Vader and Lord Voldemort. He pushed open the door and stepped inside.

"It's okay, you lot. You can follow me now," he called back.

As he waited for the others to join him, Dylan took in his surroundings. At first glance, it seemed a very normal hallway in a very normal, if rather old-fashioned, house, until...

Chapter 3

"Hello! I'm George," announced an orange corgi sitting in front of a long mirror. Perched on the head of this friendly-looking dog was a blue, peaked cap with two holes for the animal's pointed ears. Across the front of the cap were the letters B-U-D-S. "They're in the kitchen. Some of your lot don't talk yet. Most of those who do are in the coal house at the back."

"My lot?" queried Dylan.

"EDDs. Earth Dimension Dogs. Scottie warned us you might be along sometime this morning with your bitch."

"My bitch? I don't have a bitch. Or any sort of dog."

"Called Alice or something?"

Dylan felt furious. He was just about to say a very rude word when Alice appeared in the doorway, followed by Caitlin and Ben.

"Glad to see you're not a duck," Alice joked. "I did worry about you. A bit."

She worried about me? Wow, man! But only a bit?

"Is this her?" asked George.

"Oh, not another talking dog! Hello!" remarked Alice, looking down. "So... who are you?"

"George. And you must be his bit—"

"Alice is my neighbour," interrupted Dylan. "That's her brother Ben, and the girl in red's my baby sister, Caitlin."

Caitlin was already preening herself in the mirror, running her fingers through her long, flowing hair, seeing what it looked like both in front of, and behind her shoulders.

"Hey, enough of that baby business, brother. Ben, wouldn't you like to see my red—?"

"Where's Bouncer?" Dylan asked George, determined to play the dutiful brother and keep the lid on his precocious young sister. "Alice simply has to see him. Now!"

"Stop interrupting me, Dylan. I want to show Ben my red brooch!"

"Oh, sorry. I thought you meant something else."

"Oh, brothers!" exclaimed Caitlin. She unclasped a red brooch pinned to the front of her dress. Being a similar red, it didn't show up very well. "When I complained about brothers, I wasn't including you, Ben. Alice is so lucky to have one like you."

Dylan felt a prick of shame pierce where it hurt. Caitlin, like himself, was clever and, in many ways, including her looks, his superior. Thank goodness, he would soon be sixteen to keep an edge of seniority in their relationship.

Caitlin handed the brooch to Ben who grinned whilst examining it.

"Where did you get this?" he asked.

"My dad. When he went to Hong Kong. For a maths conference. He's brilliant, you know. The Chinese asked him to go there. Something about a new way of teaching maths for people who find it hard. They thought he was the best person to show them."

Dylan wished she would shut up about their father who had come so close to destroying his chances of ever winning the love of the Chinese girl standing beside him.

"What does it say?" Caitlin asked.

"The characters, they say—" Ben held it up for Caitlin to see. She came up close (*very* close) whilst he pointed to the characters as he read them out: *"Zhù nǐ hǎo yùn."*

"What's that mean?" she asked.

"It means 'wish you good luck', Caitlin. Your father wants you always to have good luck. Like you said, red is a lucky colour."

"I want *you* to have it."

"No! Your father meant it for his precious daughter."

"Then keep it safe for me. For as long as you want. It doesn't show on this dress, anyway, being red." Ben frowned. He looked doubtful. "Please!" insisted Dylan's sister. "That way both of us might be lucky."

"Okay!" agreed Ben, slipping the brooch into his pocket. "I'll look after it for you. Just for now. But you really shouldn't—"

"Bouncer will be with the other dogs," George interrupted. "Either in the kitchen or the coal house. Better hurry. *He* will be here very soon."

"You mean the professor?" asked Dylan.

"Uh-huh! You know, but for him she might languish in jail for the rest of her life. What remains of it."

Dylan glanced at Alice. "*She* being?" he asked.

"His owner. Bosona. Look, just go along that corridor and through into the kitchen where the EDDs, your Earth dogs, can get a drink of cambo juice. This changes their voice boxes to Dogtopian mode. If he's not there, go out through the back door and cross the lawn to the coal house. Not difficult, even for a human."

"Dogtopian?"

"A dimension beyond the time-space scrambler. In the coal house."

"Just a minute. 'Not difficult even for a human'? Isn't Professor Pringle human? And clever? We're not all stupid, you know." He wanted to say, 'Like Colin McPhail,' but thought that would be testing his luck with Alice a step too far.

"If you young humans went to school, maybe you'd be a bit brighter. Why don't you, if you can talk?"

"I *do* go to school. With Alice."

"With your bit—?"

"*And* he always comes top in class," Alice added just in time. "Top in everything, actually."

Dylan's confidence tree shot up to elm sized. A very red tree, too, for he felt his face go hot.

"Came from Earth originally, some reckon!" announced George. "The professor, that is. There are those who believe he's almost as clever as us dogs. Whatever… he invented the Vortex."

"The what?"

"Vortex. Time-space scrambler. Great Dog, if you're the cleverest in your school, what on earth are the others like?"

Dylan thought again of Colin and his dumb face and hoped that Alice wasn't thinking about the rugby dude's muscles.

"How are we gonna get to Bouncer before they put him in that Vortex thing?" the girl asked. "I wish—" she began, then looked at Dylan and went silent.

Wishes Colin were here instead? But would he have dared enter Number Twenty-four alone? Dylan may have been skinny, but he did not lack courage.

"Stay put," he said to Alice. "I'll find him for you. Ben will look after you, won't you, Ben?

"Shan't let my little sister out of my sight," replied the older boy.

"What about me?" asked Caitlin.

"Stay with Ben, too. If I'm not back in five minutes, send a search party."

"A search party?" Caitlin queried. She looked around the hallway. "What search party?"

"You," replied her brother. Before she could respond, Dylan walked with determination towards a door at the far end of the corridor, and towards the sound of barking and shouting. He hesitated before opening it.

"Go on!" George stood behind him, no longer wagging his tail. "They won't bite. Unless you annoy them."

Scottie remained in the hallway with the others.

What if they've kidnapped Bouncer? Perhaps, Dylan wondered, *these dogs aren't so friendly after all.* Then he thought of Alice and Colin together. He opened the door to the kitchen.

The room was full of dogs. Every breed, shape and size imaginable. In fact, Dylan reckoned most of the dogs in the Scottish Borders, apart from Bouncer, must have been squeezed into that kitchen filled to near eardrum-bursting with the noise of shouting and barking. A large Alsatian bounded up to Dylan.

"Where's the professor?" it asked in a gruff voice. "We've almost run out of cambo juice."

Dylan shrugged his shoulders. There were a few dog bowls on the floor, each the size of a kitchen sink, and all but one empty.

"This human here is looking for Bouncer," George answered on the boy's behalf. "His bitch is Bouncer's pet."

"Alice is not a bitch! She's very nice. And kind to Bouncer. Anyway, she's not 'mine'. Where is he?"

"Gone through," replied the Alsatian.

"To the coal house? Fine, I'll go get him!" said Dylan.

"Not a good idea. They've started up the Vortex already. No telling where you might end up. Bouncer's probably already passed over. He's really bright, they say."

"They?"

"Charlie and Spots. Tested all of us. Apparently, Bouncer's our best Earth dimension dog ever. They've made him a captain already, so he had to pass through with the first lot."

"To Dogtopia?"

"We hope so. Charlie told me there's always an element of doubt. Wouldn't want to end up in Dinoverse," he said. Dylan most definitely did not want Alice to end up as *T. Rex* food if she were to join him.

"Scottie promised she'd be able to see Bouncer again," the boy insisted. "I can't let her down. Not today. There's a rugby match tomorrow and Colin will be showing off his frigging muscles."

"Oh, Scottie's always promising things he doesn't know anything about. Is Colin a dog? Where we're going, we could do with a dog with muscles."

"Worse than a dog. He's a threat to civilization! Look, couldn't you just go to the coal house for me and see if Bouncer's there? I promise that, one day, Alice will give you enough prawn crackers to fill a—fill a bloody kennel!"

The Alsatian studied Dylan for a few moments with his head to one side. He turned and pushed his way through the canine medley to converse with a droopy-eared Dalmatian. He seemed to be chewing the spotted dog's ear until it became clear to the boy that he was whispering something. The Dalmatian looked back at him just as a loud scream from the hallway cut, like a knife, through the barking and jabbering. A sudden hush descended on the kitchen but the screaming from the hallway continued.

Dylan's ears were well-tuned to the screams of his little sister. He'd have recognized that sound a mile away, let alone from just along the corridor, and it almost drowned the panic-stricken shouts of the Chinese brother and sister. And the voice of a man.

Oh my God, the professor!

The screams pierced through to the boy's brain cells where, suddenly, Caitlin's safety was even more important to him than finding Bouncer. Although she could be intensely annoying, she was, after all, still his little sister. Besides, if something should happen to her, who could he be rude to? Dylan nudged aside a dozy spaniel and ran back along the corridor. The screaming had ceased, and when he reached the hallway, Alice stood there alone, trembling.

"Where's Caitlin?" he asked.

"Duck!" the girl replied. "Duck! That man... he said—then... duck!"

Dylan heard quacking upstairs. Alice clapped her hand to her mouth. Those lovely eyes were now so wide the boy feared they might pop out.

"Where's Ben?" he asked. The girl, seemingly unable to utter another word, pointed upwards. Dylan ran to the bottom of the stairs. Halfway up were Caitlin's red party dress, her bra and her knickers, red as she had informed everyone. Angered at seeing these discarded, he bounded up, two stairs at a time, to find Ben standing at an open doorway. The quacking had stopped. The only sounds were those of Alice's sobs from the hallway below and the more distant noise of barking and shouting that had resumed in the kitchen. Now less barking and more shouting. Dylan joined Ben who stood looking out at a black, empty space.

"Where's Caitlin? What's happened to my sister?"

"A man in a black cloak. No face. Just red eyes. He grabbed her. Then she changed. Turned into a—a cute little... you know. Quacking thing. He said she must remain a—" Ben went silent.

"What? What did the professor say?"

The Chinese boy continued to stare at nothing as if searching for a word to complete the sentence. Dylan knew the answer before it got spelt out. The thing that terrified all the children of Hawick from P1 up:

Duck!

"He said as a pretty little duck she would serve his purpose better. Because of her hair. That was the strange thing. A duck with a tuft of red hair. I tried to stop him, but he was too quick. Just opened this door here and jumped out holding a quacking Caitlin. Or rather, a duck."

This cannot be happening. Am I still dreaming?

Dylan's mind flashed back to a heavenly dream, interrupted by his alarm clock early that morning, in which he had been kissing the Chinese boy's sister.

"I'm going after them," Ben said, turning and looking Dylan straight in the eye.

"You what?" Dylan stared beyond the older boy at the black emptiness beyond. He tried to make out shapes and patterns, but his eyes only came up with... with nothing! "You can't. There's nothing there. Not even a dark room." He tapped at the void with his foot. "Or a floor!"

"I don't care. I can't let anything happen to your sister."

"It already has. She's a duck."

Dylan felt awful. Even his sister's incessant jibes were better than having her quack all the time. Ben slipped his hand into his pocket and took out Caitlin's brooch. He gazed at it for a few moments.

"It just might be lucky. Who knows? Look after Alice for me."

"No!" cried Dylan, but he was too late. The Chinese boy returned the brooch to his pocket, stepped over the brink and vanished.

Downstairs, it was deathly quiet.

Alice?

"Alice!" he shouted, afraid that she too might have been transformed into something else. No reply. Gripped by panic, he turned and ran downstairs, briefly stopping half-way to pick up his sister's dress and underwear. Thank goodness Alice was still there, her hand cupped over her mouth, staring in horror at an old, white-haired man silhouetted in the open front doorway. Scottie stood beside the shabby fellow, furiously wagging his tail.

A fuse burst somewhere in Dylan's brain. His sister had, in his head, been turned back into the cute, curly-red-haired child with whom he used to play so happily in the park before her critical faculties started to grow out of proportion to her age. He ran at the professor and beat the man on the chest with both fists.

"Bring my sister back, you bastard! And not as a flipping duck!"

"A *flipping* duck?" queried the old man.

"Aye, a *flipping* duck! You've no right to turn her into a *flipping* duck. With red hair, too. Even if she can be annoying."

"A red-haired, flipping duck? Oh dear, oh dear! This sounds bad."

"Yes, it is, you great bully!"

"Dylan!"

"What?" The boy turned to face Alice. "I'm gonna knock his head off if he doesn't bring Caitlin back."

"Dylan, this isn't the same man."

Dylan spun back round to take in the old man. He'd only seen the professor once before. Although the name Professor Pringle was known to all neighbourhood children, of late a 'professor sighting' had been rare and worthy of a Snapchat posting. Most of the time, Number Twenty-four remained shut up, as if nobody had lived there for years. Then someone would catch a glimpse of the bent, wrinkled old fellow with his untidy mop of white hair and eyes that twinkled like stars. Word would quickly spread:

"The professor's back," got passed from child to child. "Oooh—quack, quack!" some would respond. And now Dylan stood before the ancient academic. Nearly sixteen, the boy was several inches taller.

"What do you mean, Alice? This is the professor. I recognize him. Saw him once before. And now he's gone and stolen my sister. What the heck am I gonna say to Mum and Dad?"

"Well he's not the man who changed Caitlin into a duck. He was—sort of—"

"Black cloak and hood? Red eyes like burning coals?" queried Professor Pringle.

Alice nodded.

"That's him all right!"

"Who?"

"Scissorman. Uses his fingers like scissors. They can cut through threads that link us to the reality we're in. Those clothes you're holding, Dylan. Do they belong to your sister?"

"You know my name?" There was absolutely no reason for this old man to know his name.

"Of course!"

Dylan looked despairingly at the dress, the red knickers and the bra in his hand. Tears welled, and he fought to stop them getting any further because, of all things, he could not let Alice see him cry. Not even over his little sister.

"Yes, they're hers," he replied, turning his face away from the girl. "Why?"

"Might help us get your sister back. Keep them safe."

Hmm! thought Dylan. *It's all she'll have to wear if we ever find her again.* He retrieved his rucksack from where he'd dropped it, pricked by remorse as he pushed in Caitlin's dress and underwear. He couldn't understand why this made him feel both angry and sad.

"Ben's got her lucky red Chinese brooch," he told the professor.

"Good. And where's Ben?" Dylan avoided looking at Alice. How on earth was he going to tell her? "Is he clever, by the way?" enquired the professor.

Alice nodded.

"Yes. Like Dylan." Dylan's face pinkened again. "He's going to Edinburgh Uni after the summer. To study medicine. He's always wanted to be a doctor."

"And I'm gonna be a vet!" exclaimed Dylan, more for Alice's benefit than the professor's.

"You haven't answered my question. Where is Ben?"

Dylan looked down at the floor. It hurt too much to look at the girl whilst saying the words:

"He went through that door upstairs."

"The one on the left?" queried the professor.

"The one on the left."

"Hasn't been opened for years. Oh dear, this is serious. Scissorman's going to use her. And the boy too, maybe. But particularly her, being a duck with red hair as I understand it. You really saw Ben go through that door?"

"What door?" asked Alice. "Oh, please tell him to come down here, Dylan. With the duck. I mean your sister. She can put those clothes back on and we'll all just go ho—"

"Alice, it's not that simple," interrupted the professor. "Come here, my child."

Alice looked sideways at Dylan, but he avoided her gaze. He was a hopeless liar. Caitlin was always telling him that. Professor Pringle took Alice's hands in his.

"Your brother must be extremely brave, but he's done a very silly thing. He's stepped into the Interim."

"The what?"

"Interim. Think of it as a no-man's land between different realities. Or different dimensions. (He glanced at Dylan.) If you're into science. Scissorman can manipulate it by using his fingers. Guess you'd call it 'magic' if you're not into science. Even I cannot travel across the Interim. That's why I invented the Vortex. Over the past few decades, he's taken a few changed children to Duckdom via the Interim. Got a good price for them, probably."

"Duckdom?"

"A place identical to earth where ducks, not humans, are in charge." The thought of Caitlin lording it over Dylan as a duck was worse than her teasing him as a thirteen-year-old schoolgirl. "Unfortunately, that's not where Scissorman plans to take Caitlin. She'll end up in Dogtopia Palace. Because of what's happening there."

"A palace? She always wanted to be a princess living in a palace. I used to read to her a lot when she was little, you know," Dylan informed Alice. "About princesses and stuff."

"But not ducks," emphasized the professor. "Oh dear, oh dear... the Interim! Let's hope Ben truly is clever. The fact that Scissorman showed up here today is deeply disturbing. One of our own dogs must have betrayed Bosona's cause."

"Who's Bosona?" asked Dylan.

Before the old man could reply, Alice ran to the stairs. "I want to see for myself," she sobbed. "Ben would never leave me like this!"

"No!" shouted Dylan. He rushed after her. The door upstairs was still open, and he managed to grab her just in time. He held firmly on to the girl as she cried out into the void: "Ben, Ben... come back! Please! I can't live without you!"

The professor had followed them up to the landing.

"It's no use, my child," he said. "Wherever your brother is now, he'll most certainly not hear you. There's only one way, and who knows, if Dylan and Ben really are clever it may just turn out to be for the best?" When she turned to face the man, the anger in her face took Dylan by surprise. Anger and tears did not suit her.

"How can this be for the best?" she sobbed.

"In *my* world. Dogtopia. You asked me who Bosona is. She's my owner. The rightful Top Dog. I, the great Professor Pringle, am her pet."

***

Ben began to wonder about the purpose of his life to date as he spun in all directions, unable to feel, see or hear anything. That morning, life had changed beyond recognition. He'd been awoken by his little sister creeping around, seen her leave the house, and, wanting to help her get Bouncer back if what the boy next door had said was true, had quickly dressed and followed her. Caitlin obviously had similar thoughts, though for a different reason. One that pricked him with guilt. She had always made her infatuation with Ben painfully obvious, and emerged, looking embarrassed, from her front door moments after Ben. She nodded when Ben asked her whether Dylan had also just left the house. Then things got stranger and stranger. First a talking dog, followed by his nerdy neighbour's little sister getting changed into a duck, and now here he was floating free range in space.

Weird, or weirder than weird? And if I never live to become a doctor, it's all been a waste of time, he thought. *Plus, I'll never get to give Alice that present I've saved up to buy her for her sixteenth birthday. Those shoes we saw in Edinburgh and Mum said they were too grownup because of the high heels and Alice was really upset. She'll not get those shoes if I don't stay alive. And poor little Caitlin might remain a duck forever and ever. So—just gotta work this out! First... stop spinning!*

Ben and his dad practised *Tai Chi* together every morning. He was good at it, his dad told him. A natural. It was all about control, so, muscle by muscle, he began to control his limbs and stop the spinning. In this way, he became an object with direction. He found himself shooting through space head-first, like a human arrow.

As with those who master *Tai Chi*, arrows have direction and purpose. Someone aims at a target with his or her bow, and the arrow is destined to strike its mark if that purpose is met. Hopefully, the bullseye. His purpose, right now, was to find Caitlin and turn her back into a girl. His hand reached into his pocket, and his fingers closed around Caitlin's lucky brooch. The arrow slowed. Everything brightened, and detail started to appear in the upside-down horizon. Hills and trees now hung from it.

"Not a good idea to hit the ground at the speed of a meteorite," his mind told his brain. *Tai Chi* took over. He flipped himself around and, by clutching the brooch even more tightly, he discovered he could slow down, like pressing his foot on a brake pedal. He landed upright, as if he'd just jumped off a two-foot wall. The problem now was that the place where he had landed was totally alien. A large palace, perched on a solitary mountain in the distance, was unlike anything he had seen in the Scottish Borders or near his relatives in China. But of one thing he felt certain: Caitlin had been taken to that palace. The brooch told him this.

***

Alice, still crying, allowed Dylan to place a comforting arm across her shoulders as they followed the professor back downstairs. He hoped this might soften the anger in her eyes. The corgi was waiting for them in the hallway.

"He's passed over," George said.

"Who?" asked the professor.

"Her owner. Bouncer. Spots said they couldn't wait any longer, what with Bouncer being a captain. The goldador was very upset, actually. Said he so wanted to say goodbye to her. Seems she's been a really good pet for him."

"Will Bouncer find Ben for me?" questioned Alice. "And Dylan's sister?"

Professor Pringle shrugged his shoulders. He looked from Alice to Dylan. The boy saw a deeply troubled mind behind the ancient lines furrowing his forehead, and he realised that there were no easy answers to the girl's questions.

"D'you have enough power left in the Vortex for two extra humans?" the old man asked George.

"Probably."

"Only probably?"

"They're not small. Plus, the girl's quite uptight. That'll need more energy. But there'll be a pull from the other end because Bouncer wants to see her. Her brother too, probably. If he's there. And the other girl won't be too happy about being a duck. So, all in all…"

"We have to try. No time to boot another power pack. Take them to the coal house. I'll be along later. With the last lot of Earth dogs. Alice, we'll do everything we can."

Alice, now beyond tears, just looked at the professor with those fascinating brown oriental eyes that, for Dylan, set her apart from all other girls in their S4 class at Hawick High School. And it seemed to the boy that the hopes, prayers, trust and wishes of all humanity were concentrated in those beautiful eyes that morning.

I'll find Ben and Caitlin if it's the last thing I ever do! he vowed.

The kitchen was empty, as was the large bowl of cambo juice. Dylan opened the back door and Alice followed him and George into the garden. The boy halted.

"Isn't Scottie coming?" he asked. The little white dog remained at the kitchen door, wagging his tail.

"Not Scottie! He stays behind nowadays," George replied. "Enjoys pretending to be an Earth dog. Has an outside kennel here, so he comes and goes as he pleases. Convenient for the professor, too. Scottie's new pets—or owners, as you lot would have it—are a couple of kids. They play football with him. He has a pretty good time. You see, at least one of us must stay behind. To get more recruits for Bosona."

Dylan shrugged his shoulders and, together with Alice and George, headed through knee-high grass for a wooden building at the back of the large garden, half-hidden by overgrown laurel bushes. George pushed open the coal house door with a paw.

"Oh, there's just one thing. If you're lucky enough to survive the passing over. Do not let the Wolf Police know you can talk," he informed the two teens.

"Wolf Police?"

"Brutal! You'll get tortured for information if they know you understand speech. Just behave like normal humans and 'woof'."

"I can't woof," said Alice. "And it's *not* normal for humans!" Dylan sensed a return of girlish annoyance.

"Well, it is in Dogtopia. Either you try, or we'll have to give you cambo juice," George warned with a mischievous glint in his eye. "But then you'd not be able to talk at all!" Dylan reckoned he had enough problems communicating with his pretty neighbour without having her woof like a dog.

"Just try," he pleaded. "Like this: Ra! Ra!"

After a few feeble woofs, Alice managed to make an almost dog-like sound. They followed George into a room at the back of the coal house where two scruffy brown mongrels lay stretched out on the floor beside a contraption that looked like a vast spin drier. Up against this was a short step ladder. A large silver tube connected the Vortex with a rust-pocked black cabinet dotted with illuminated dials, knobs, switches and levers. Dylan wished the professor would reappear and take control, for he felt uneasy about entrusting his and Alice's lives to the hands, or rather paws, of a podgy little corgi called George, even if the dog was wearing a cap with a badge.

"What does B... U.... D.... S. stand for?" he asked.

"Bosona's Ultimate Dog Squad. Of which you two humans are now honorary members. I hope those caps aren't too big." The corgi's nose indicated two baseball caps lying on the floor beside the Vortex. "They belonged to a couple of Great Danes who lost their lives in battle." Alice and Dylan looked at each other. It was rapidly sinking in. This would be more than just another school outing. They might die. Dylan wished he could reassure the girl, for finding Bouncer now seemed the least of her problems, but fear rendered him speechless.

The blue caps, rather large, had holes on the top to allow for canine ears. They looked very peculiar on their heads. The mongrels got up and, wagging their tails, waddled over to the girl and boy.

"We're twins," they said together. "Our Earth pets call us Bill and Ben," one informed them. "They live on a farm just outside Hawick," said the other. "George says we should help you if you help us," added the first.

"Help you do what?" Alice asked.

"Free Bosona!"

Chapter 4

"I'm Bill," said the larger of the mongrels. "I'll go first in case of trouble at the other end. You two can travel together afterwards. If you can squeeze in. Better that way in case you end up somewhere else."

"Like Dinoverse?" queried Dylan. His voice had turned almost helium balloon squeaky.

"If you're lucky. But it's not gonna happen. Not if you've got a lot of purpose in you." Like Alice with her brother, Dylan now desperately wanted his little sister back. "My brother Ben can follow," continued Bill. "and Scottie will send George later. Now watch carefully. One foot wrong, and not even dinosaurs would be able to do much with what comes out the other end."

Alice started to tremble. Dylan took hold of her hand again and gave it a gentle squeeze. Somehow, he got away with this. She didn't even frown.

"We'll be okay," he whispered. "Just listen to Bill."

The mongrel scrambled up the steps and stood perched on a platform at the top of the Vortex. His twin sat in front of the cabinet and tapped a winking green button with his paw. The machine whirred, then a circular door sprang open.

"There are two seats inside. Strap yourselves in and pull the masks over your faces. These will drop down as soon as you're secured."

Dylan recalled a similar instruction, on a flight to Tenerife, should the airplane fall out of the sky. Caitlin, beside him at the time, had asked what she should do if the mask didn't fit. Thinking of Caitlin gave him courage.

"Keep your rucksack between your feet, Dylan," instructed Bill. "Don't say a word when the time-space scrambler starts up. And most important of all, do *not* scream." That was one thing the boy had never done, but he couldn't account for Alice. "It's not that bad, really. Close your eyes if you must. Most first-timers do. But humans who open them can enjoy lots of pretty patterns. And colours. That's what the professor says, anyway."

Dylan remembered reading, somewhere, how dogs see colours differently. If he were to keep his eyes open, he could tell Alice about it. She might even consider him brave.

"There's a lever in between the seats. It's a brake. When the noise goes quieter, start to pull this back. Slowly and carefully, so that the sound stays the same. And only pull it right back when the humming stops altogether. Got it?"

"Aye!" agreed Dylan after repeating the instructions inside his head. Alice remained silent. The boy could feel her small hand tremble in his. At last he had a chance to impress her. He hoped.

Bill jumped into the Vortex. Ben tapped a red button and the circular door snapped shut. Immediately, the strange contraption began to hum. The hum grew louder. Ben sprang into action, tapping at various buttons and levers whilst wagging his tail. It all looked a bit random, but, for Alice's sake, Dylan tried to suppress his growing fear that the dog hadn't a clue what he was doing and was merely having fun. Lights flashed and a small LED screen, which the boy noticed for the first time, displayed a countdown starting with 999. Why not a thousand, he had no idea. After a hundred, the numbers slowed, and the hum grew quieter.

"Bill's applying the brake," Ben the dog informed them.

After ten, the numbers dropped at one second intervals until... zero. The Vortex went quiet.

"He's arrived," said Ben. "Your turn now, guys."

Dylan helped Alice up the steps, then followed. They waited at the top for the circular door to flip open. After climbing in, the boy made sure that Alice was securely fastened before adjusting his own seat belt, trapping the rucksack between his feet. He was so thankful the girl hadn't teased him about the Superman image for he felt anything but 'super'. It was six years old, but there was no way his dad would buy him a new one. "I warned you you'd soon outgrow it," the man had said. "Why don't you ever listen?"

Neither Dylan nor Alice said a word. The boy reassured himself that the brake was where it should be. Alice still seemed to be in a state of shock, so it would be his job to apply it. The door above them snapped shut. A light came on.

He prayed that the girl didn't suffer from claustrophobia for there wasn't much space between them and the shiny metal wall of the Vortex. He detected fear in her eyes and smiled as best he could, hoping this might make her feel better. It didn't. Perhaps it hadn't been much of a smile. After all, he, too, was terrified out of his wits.

A hum started up and grew rapidly louder. Dylan wanted to cover his ears, but he needed one hand free. He felt again for the brake and kept his hand on it whilst preparing for entry into another dimension.

When the humming got unbearably loud, lights began to flash. Dylan expected to shake or wobble or be bumped about. Instead, everything remained strangely still. He tried smiling again at Alice. This time she smiled back, and he felt stronger. He offered her a thumbs-up with his free hand, although couldn't think why. They might yet perish.

Suddenly the flashing lights altered. They became colourful, and the colours kept changing, dappling Alice's face and the wall of the Vortex with kaleidoscopic patterns. Alice closed her eyes, but Dylan kept his open. Amongst shapes of every imaginable hue and shade were some that he recognized. A *T. Rex* floated past followed by a jumping kangaroo and, God forbid, a waddling duck. Soon the hum dropped to something like that of a distant beehive. When Dylan tried to ease the brake back, it seemed stuck.

His confidence tree shrank to a tiny green shoot. He started to sweat as the sound continued to dwindle, for the brake wouldn't budge. Something resembling a pink hippo bumbled into view. The hum was barely audible and still the brake remained jammed. Alice opened her eyes and looked at Dylan. No way could he fail her.

His fingers travelled down the brake's stem and came up against something soft and warm. It felt like fur. The fur had a tail. His fingers explored the other end till they discovered a tiny, twitching nose. He grabbed the tail and yanked a mouse free from the space between the brake and its casing, holding it up for Alice to see. She covered a grin with her hand whilst Dylan skilfully pulled back the brake halfway, now able to control the fading hum. A black and white dog zipped past.

The mouse got handed to Alice who, holding it up by the tail, giggled at the little creature. Dylan's tree grew bigger. He listened to the hum, focusing on the grip he applied to the brake as he carefully edged it further back. The flashing ceased. For a few moments they sat in pitch blackness. Dylan expected Alice to scream but she didn't.

Better trained than Caitlin, he reckoned. A soft, yellow light came on and the door above sprang open. Alice stroked the mouse whilst Dylan unfastened their belts. They heard a chatter of voices. The boy stood and poked his head up through the opening. Bill and several other dogs, all wagging their tails, greeted him with shouts and cheers:

"You're here!" announced Bill.

But where? After all that worry and panic, they seemed to be back where they had started. The coal house was unchanged, although Bill's twin, Ben-the-dog, was no longer at the controls.

"Is this some sort of a joke?" Dylan asked. He felt both angry and relieved. But relief that he was looking at dogs, not dinosaurs, was soon replaced by uncertainty. There was yapping as well as shouts and cheers, and that's when he first saw them:

The humans.

Dressed in brown tunics, they began to run around, barking with excitement. Even in Hawick, humans did not bark. Also, they were much the same size as the dogs—as were he and Alice.

Dylan climbed up onto the rim of the Vortex and waited for the ladder. Two servile humans yapped at him as they carefully propped this up against the side of the machine. The boy helped Alice out, and the mouse got passed between them as they took turns to descend the steps.

"Welcome to Dogtopia!" said Bill, at which all the dogs again cheered. Dylan was about to utter a word he shouldn't when Alice did something unexpected. She kissed him on the cheek. Definitely the best moment of his life to date!

"*Xie xie!*" she whispered.

"You're welcome!"

One day I, too, will be saying thank you in Chinese, he thought.

"What've you got in your hands, Alice?" asked Bill.

The girl showed him.

"Curse Sammy the spaniel. I don't know how many times I told him to leave the mice alone. He must've dropped it whilst passing over. Looks like we're stuck with this one."

"Does Sammy eat them?" queried Alice, frowning. She tickled the mouse's tummy.

"Plays with them. That's all."

"D'you think Caitlin would mind if we wrap him in her dress?" Alice asked Dylan. It saddened the boy to have to use his sister's dress for such a purpose, but he could think of no alternative. Better than using her knickers.

"So long as we call him 'Whiskers'," he replied before opening up his rucksack. "She used to have a soft toy mouse with pink ears and his name was 'Whiskers', you see."

"Hear that, Whiskers?" the Chinese girl whispered as she made him snug and cosy in Caitlin's dress. "And now you must help us find Ben and Caitlin."

"Ben'll be here very soon," said Bill. Alice stopped stroking Whiskers and stared at him.

"No! She means *her* Ben!" responded Dylan. "Her brother! Same name as yours."

"Oh! Nice name, I guess. Important sounding. Now remember," Bill continued, "you two can only talk in our company. And then *only* if you're certain there are no Wolf Police around." He approached the door. "Oh—and beware! Things will change once you're outside the hut."

"Change? What will change?"

"Our roles. And sizes. The professor calls it the reversal. Started already, you see."

Even though his eyes were now at the same level as Bill's, Dylan remained unconvinced that they were anywhere other than in the coal house at the back of the garden of Number Twenty-four in Hawick. When told that human/dog roles and sizes would be reversed outside, he raised his eyebrows for Alice's sake—as if to inform her not to worry because this talking dog was as daft as a fruit bat. He followed Bill outside. His grin vanished.

The boy found himself looking up at the mongrel. Bill was larger than the biggest of the horses that congregated in his hometown every summer for the Hawick Common Riding. He felt Alice search for his hand, and he locked fingers with her. Together, they stood, hand in hand, looking out over a vast, empty plain, together with a pack of giant dogs and several smaller barking humans. In the far distance was a sizeable mountain on the top of which stood a magnificent palace.

"Wow!" murmured Dylan. "Dogtopia Palace, I guess!"

Alice muttered something in Mandarin Chinese incomprehensible to Dylan. The only words of her mother tongue that he understood were 'hello' and 'thank you'. He was determined to learn more of that language should they survive. More than Colin McPhail ever could. Even to say, 'I hate haggis', in English that could be understood six miles away in Selkirk, would be a challenge for that pea-brained rugby buff.

The huge dogs were gathered in an orderly formation on the grass outside the hut. There must have been over two hundred of them, all wearing blue peaked caps with BUDS badges. A snow-white poodle with thin black lips wore hers tilted to one side. She had one of those fluffy round bobbles that well-groomed poodles often sport on the tops of their heads. This stuck out from one of the ear holes.

"Bouncer! There you are!"

Alice, who had been searching the rows of dogs, suddenly ran off, dodging tree trunk-sized dog legs till she reached the goldador. It was the weirdest thing Dylan had ever seen. So often, he had stood at his bedroom window looking down at Alice and her adored pet as they played in her garden, wishing he could join them. Now it was as though his wish had come true, only the reversed owner/pet roles added an unwelcome nuance. Bouncer looked down at Alice who stood hugging his huge paw up against her chest, his flabby, skateboard-sized tongue dangling like pink rubber sheet. For an awful moment the boy feared that Bouncer might gobble her up. His canine teeth were more like those of a sabre-toothed tiger than a normal dog. But Bouncer, being Bouncer, posed no threat. He seemed as delighted to be reunited with Alice as Dylan would have been if he were a dog. The tongue gently licked the girl before its owner squatted down for her to tickle his chin.

"Take care of your pet," George advised Bouncer. "She's a very precious human."

"You bet she's precious!" replied the goldador. "Pedigree Chinese, you know!"

Dylan approached and stood beside Alice.

"Bouncer, you must meet my friend Dylan," Alice said. "He lives next door to us."

Wow! She called me her 'friend'! But dinnae get too excited, dude. She didn't say 'boyfriend'.

"I know. I've seen him staring down at you from his upstairs window."

Alice frowned again.

"Do you spy on me?" she asked. The boy's confidence tree shrank.

"No. Um—well—I just—" He did some quick thinking as her frown darkened. "I told you I want to be a vet. Thought I could learn stuff by watching someone who really understands animals, see."

Alice smiled, thank God.

"He always comes top in our class," she informed her pet-turned-owner. Dylan was still uncertain as to whether this fact put him above or below the rugby buff Colin in the universal order of things. At least, as far as *she* was concerned. He shrugged his shoulders as though it was no big deal.

"The professor, too, says he's clever," added George who had waddled up behind them. "I'll ask the general to make him an honorary lieutenant." A more acceptable size than Bouncer, the squat corgi now resembled a large pig. "But he never said anything about the boy being a vet."

"Not yet. Not old enough," protested Dylan. "But I do want to be. One day."

"Now's your chance. We need a vet in the squad. Who knows? I wouldn't put it beyond the rotts to use chemical weapons."

Rotts? Chemical weapons? Dylan no longer felt so very clever.

The corgi wandered off to join a group of dogs surrounding an elephant-sized St Bernard. From its furry neck dangled an enormous barrel which Dylan assumed must contain brandy. It was the only dog without a cap. Instead, it wore what looked like an upturned basin. In bold red letters, it bore the word 'GENERAL'.

"General Scratch," Bouncer said on observing Dylan staring at the giant dog. "Comes from around these parts. Lost nearly all his army to the rotts. Which is why the professor came up with the idea of getting Earth dogs to join BUDS."

Dylan had a disturbing thought. He checked the weight of his rucksack. It felt the same. Thankfully, Whiskers was still a wee mouse.

"So, not all animals get bigger here, then?" he asked Bouncer. "Only dogs, I guess?"

"Don't ask me. I've only just arrived."

"Well, I've a mouse on my back. Didn't fancy it turning into a giant rat. Plus, my sister's a duck. Still normal-sized, I hope—if she really is here. That's not good, of course, but a heck of a sight better than an ostrich-sized one."

"That gorgeous red-haired girl next door? She is not a duck!" insisted Bouncer.

"Got turned into one, I'm afraid. By Scissorman."

"Oh—I've heard about him!"

"And what about the rotts? Who are they?" Alice asked.

"Ah—a different question altogether! From what I've been told, you would not want to meet one, that's for sure," her owner replied.

"You mentioned someone called Bosona. Professor Pringle said he's Bosona's pet. What does he mean?" asked Dylan. Bouncer raised his head and peered around, as if to check that no other dog ears were trained on them.

"Follow me," he said. He got up and walked to the back of the coal house, even though the other dogs were too busy chattering amongst themselves to pay attention to him. Dylan reckoned they were probably making up for all those years on Earth spent barking about nothing in particular. He and Alice followed the girl's owner.

"Bit more private here," whispered Bouncer. "George told me about a possible traitor in our midst. I have my suspicions. Yes, the professor is Bosona's pet. She's Top Dog, you see. Under her rule, it used to be a great place to live, they say. Not so wonderful for humans, perhaps, but Bosona's laws made sure dogs were kind to animals."

"Animals?"

"Humans, mostly. Plus, you humans are useful. Because of your hands. Do all the building, work the machines, look after poultry—"

"Ducks?" queried Dylan.

"Sure. And chickens and pigs. A few cows too, I hear. As you lot can't speak—I mean, not you and Dylan, Alice, but Dogtopian humans—there are no fights or arguments amongst your kind."

Dylan felt cross.

"You mean to say humans here are treated like slaves? For the dogs?"

"No idea what a slave is."

"Do we—rather *they*—get paid?"

"No money in Dogtopia! Just bones and stuff."

"Slaves, then! Maybe your lot need civilising. Alice, perhaps we should—"

"Oh, do let Bouncer speak... please!"

Dylan shut up like a clam.

"As I was saying," continued the goldador, "they had a very happy, *civilised* society (a large dog eye settled meaningfully on Dylan) until a bully of a rottweiler called Bruiser got appointed to chief of the Wolf Police. George says the wolves were never really to be trusted before this, but a wise old Great Dane, Danny, used to keep them under control. As Chief of Police. Then about six months ago, Danny mysteriously vanished.”

“Bruiser?”

“George thinks so, though they never found Danny’s body. Bruiser appeared from nowhere. Some say he must’ve come from Earth and learned ‘bad ways’ from you Earth humans.”

“Bad ways?”

“Not Alice, of course. I told George she’s the best pet ever. I mean other humans. Like those guys back in your place who argue and fight and shoot each other. And the Americans in Ben’s movies that he watches.” Dylan pictured Colin charging around a rugby field brandishing an AK-47. “Apparently, never in Dogtopia had they known a dog quite like Bruiser. Then more and more rotts appeared. No one can say exactly where they all came from. Under Bosona’s nose, so to speak, one by one, the staff in the castle were replaced by rotts. Loyal canines just disappeared. Dogs who’d always respected Bosona, and honoured the Great Dog—”

“Great Dog?”

“He who gave life to all dogs. And who rules in Dogeaven.”

“Like Dog heaven?”

“Shhh!” admonished Alice.

“As I was saying,” continued Bouncer, “the loyal guard dogs had all gone and rotts took their places. They got the best jobs in Dogville. On the farms, too. Everywhere, I was told!”

“Dogs running farms?” questioned Dylan.

"Please, just listen to Bouncer!" scolded Alice. Dylan turned pink.

"Bosona made a fatal error. She gave her pet, Professor Pringle, the only talking human in Dogtopia, the job of Chief Minister." Dylan so wanted to impress Alice by suggesting that this, for Dogtopian dogs, must have seemed like the Roman Emperor Caligula making his horse a senator, but courage failed him.

"None of the other humans can speak, then?" the girl asked.

"Here humans are only supposed to woof. But Bosona knew Pringle was particularly clever. She had him helping her scientists with 'passing over' experiments. It's how he arrived here from Hawick in the first place. By using crystal. From a place called South America, back on Earth, he said. He took control of the project and invented the time-space scrambler. Called it the Vortex. Crosses different dimensions. Not even Clever Dick George knows how it works. The professor returned to human Earth and got his job back as a top professor in Edinburgh University—"

"That's where Ben's going next year, right?" Dylan asked Alice.

"Shhh! I mean, yes. Bouncer, you said 'got his job back'. Like the professor was around before in Hawick. But I suppose him being away working on the Vortex gave Bruiser the chance."

"Chance to what?" asked Dylan.

"Spread lies about Pringle," answered Bouncer. "And lies that Bosona was in league with talking humans from a different dimension. That the professor was going to teach our humans to talk and take over Dogtopia. All nonsense, of course. Pringle was only finding out stuff that might help us improve things for all dogs. George said he tried to warn the general, but the old fellow's a bit deaf and, with him being so big, George couldn't get close enough to his ears."

"Warn him about what?"

"A coup."

"Like a military take over?" asked Dylan.

"That's what coup means, doesn't it?" Alice retorted sharply. Dylan fell silent again.

A scuffling sound distracted Bouncer. The goldador sniffed the air, then shuffled along on his belly to the corner of the coal house. From here, he peered out, then laughed. The first time Dylan had heard a dog laugh properly, and it made him want to giggle—something he just managed to suppress, fearing Alice would think it disrespectful. Annoyingly, she seemed to hang on to every word coming out of her owner's huge mouth.

"Only a couple of Dogtopian humans," Bouncer said. "Shoo! Be good boys, now!" Dylan heard barking. He and Alice joined Bouncer.

Two humans, young males, stood barking at Alice's owner. They were dressed in brown tunics tied with string around the waist, like the guy who had passed by Dylan's front gate on Tuesday. For the first time, the boy felt truly scared. *What if Alice gets changed into one of those? Scissorman has already turned Caitlin into a duck.*

Bouncer shooed the humans away then turned to face Alice.

"Yes, a military coup," he said. "Between them, the rotts and the wolves killed nearly all General Scratch's troops. The general escaped. Too big for them, I guess. But Bosona was captured and imprisoned in the palace dungeon."

Alice no longer appeared to be listening. She stood staring at the two men as they ran off.

"Can't they talk at all?" she asked.

"Could *I* talk when things were the other way around and I was your pet?"

The girl shook her head.

"It's just so sad," she said. "People who only bark."

"Did you think it sad when I couldn't talk to you back in Hawick?"

Alice frowned a little, then grinned.

"I'm just so pleased you can now. I was always talking to you and you'd only wag your tail. This is so much better!"

"Well, be careful you take nothing to drink here from anyone you don't trust. Could contain cambo juice. I really don't want my pet to end up barking like I used to."

And neither did Dylan.

"So, the Rotts took over after putting Bosona in prison?" the boy asked.

"Uh-huh! That was six months ago. Bruiser appointed himself Top Dog. And it's gone from bad to worse. They've brought in wolves from the wilderness. Vicious creatures who could snap your head off with one bite. A lot of humans lost theirs."

"Heads?"

Dylan took hold of Alice's hand on seeing the look on her face. He could tell she hated violence. This was his one ray of hope if she were ever to see Colin play rugby. That creep's muscles had a price attached to them.

***

Ben (the boy) dipped a hand into his pocket, feeling for Caitlin's brooch. He absent-mindedly twiddled this round and round whilst scanning the horizon on either side of the

Palace Mountain and noticed that when his fingers and the brooch made contact, he somehow knew that Caitlin was up there on that mountain. On releasing the brooch, he had no feeling for where she was. He took out the brooch and studied it, hoping to see a tiny screen or some sort of a map, for it seemed to act like a sat nav and might, he reckoned, be his only chance of finding her. But all he saw was a simple red brooch with Chinese characters. Evidently his imagination was playing games. Nevertheless, it was all he had to guide him.

Ben returned the brooch to his pocket and peered at the strange land where he now stood. He was a mere stone's throw from a forest that stretched to the horizon in both directions. Opposite the forest, and to the right of the Palace Mountain, the horizon could have been drawn with a ruler it was that straight, whereas on looking to the left, Ben saw, in the distance, a string of humpy hills undulating the plain as far as the mountain. Like the forest, those hills might give protection, he reckoned. To cut across the flat, open plain could be tantamount to suicide.

Protection? Against what? And whom?

The boy ran to the forest. It was dense. There were no paths, but so long as he remained close to the edge, and kept the mountain within his sights, he would be able to reach the hills, and from there, hopefully, the palace. Of one thing he felt certain: as well as Caitlin, there would be dogs in this alien place.

Ben did not share his sister's love of dogs. Nor of animals in general. He didn't dislike them, but he was wary. For good reason. When little, whilst visiting grandparents in rural China, he'd been bitten by a dog. He was forced to overcome his dog phobia on seeing how desperately keen his young sister was to have a puppy, but Bouncer was Alice's pet, not his. Here, he had no intention of being bitten again, and the fir trees provided a possible solution. He broke off a long straight branch and, with the aid of a sharp-edged flint, he fashioned a pointed spear. Thus armed, Ben set off toward the hills.

Unlike the silent, open plain, there were noises in the forest. Bird calls, the occasional distant cry or grunt of some hidden creature and, more alarmingly, the odd rustle or two. Close by. Spear in hand, Ben kept going, following the edge of the forest until a certain sound stopped him short:

Barking.

It came from just ahead. Ben hid behind the trunk of a tree and waited. The barking continued, getting closer. There were voices. Not speaking in English. Nor Chinese. It was an odd, guttural language that he had never heard before. Suddenly, two bearded men appeared in a small clearing. Thankfully, unarmed. But when they barked at him, Ben nearly dropped his spear. Moments later, two enormous wolves, straight out of a horror movie, broke through the undergrowth. Twice the height of the men, they panted and slavered until one spoke to its companion in that same rasping language, and the speaker's teeth resembled curvy Sinbad the Sailor daggers.

Ben's brain focused again on *tai-chi*, something he and Mr Chang did together every day. He'd also had a few lessons in *kung fu* from his dad who told him how *tai-chi* is really a martial art form. Statue-still, he relaxed every muscle in his body, concentrating on the measured flow of air through his mouth—in... out... in... out—whilst praying that the talking wolves would not pick up his scent.

The humans' darting eyes seemed to scour the forest. For a few awful seconds, one of the men appeared to be staring straight at Ben's tree, barely large enough to conceal him. One sign of movement and he would be spotted. Then, to the boy's horror, the rustling he'd heard earlier started up again. Right behind him. Ben knew he was about to die and was so sorry he would never have the chance to be a doctor and help sick people. He closed his eyes, expecting dental daggers to dig deep into his flesh any moment.

But this didn't happen.

"Long live Bosona!" someone shouted. Something large rushed past, uprooting a small tree. The barking resumed but sounded different. Ben sensed fear in the barks. He opened his eyes and, from the cover of his tree trunk, saw a vast Alsatian leap at one of the wolves, gripping its throat between powerful jaws. The humans, still barking, ran off whilst the other wolf circled around the tussling pair. It spat foreign words at the Alsatian before snapping at the dog's legs.

No time to think! Ben stepped aside, took aim and hurled his spear at the circling wolf. The weapon pierced the animal's chest. The creature screamed and leapt back. The spear dangled and danced as the wolf spun round to face Ben. Never had the boy seen such evil as in that beast's eyes. It growled a string of scrambled words and he guessed these referred to the unpleasant things it was about to do. But the wolf wasn't the only one interested in him. The Alsatian quickly twisted the neck of the creature caught in his jaws, rendering it limp and lifeless. As the other wolf sank onto its belly, muttering unintelligible curses and preparing to pounce on Ben, the Alsatian, in a single bound, was on top of it. It was a veritable battle of Titans. Before the Alsatian finally sank its teeth into the wolf's neck, he shouted:

"Bosona forever!"

Ben remained stock still when the Alsatian left the bloodied body of his second victim and approached him.

"Good boy," the dog said. "I guess you belong to one of our resistance fighters. I wonder where your master's got to. Not killed by those wolves, I hope."

"I haven't got a master."

"Wait a minute—you can speak? Like the professor?"

"I'm here to rescue a girl who got turned into a duck. I come from Hawick."

"Where?"

"Hawick. In the Scottish Borders. Only I'm Chinese. Like my sister, of course."

Ben felt confused. He had never, before, had a conversation with a normal dog, let alone a giant one. Alice often spoke to Bouncer, but Ben didn't see the point in this since Bouncer couldn't talk back to her.

"Are you with us? With Bosona?" asked the Alsatian. Ben reckoned there could only be one survivable answer to this question. He had already seen what the huge Alsatian did to a couple of mega-wolves.

"Yes, of course I am," he replied, not knowing who on Earth (*Earth?*) Bosona was.

"I'm Ali. And you?"

"Ben."

The boy wasn't prepared for what happened next. A nose the size of a dinner plate sniffed his body and face before he got licked all over by a large wet pink rug of a tongue. He wasn't sure whether this was better or worse than being bitten by a normal-sized dog in China.

"Well, they say a human is a dog's best friend, Ben. May I call you my pet? Never had one before."

Ben decided it would be wise to allow Ali to call him anything he wished. Besides, with a master like Ali, he stood a far better chance of rescuing wee Caitlin.

Chapter 5

"The general wants to see you."

The black and ginger face of an enormous Doberman had just appeared from around the corner of the coal house. It blinked at Dylan with a large brown eye.

"Me?" queried the boy. He glanced sideways at Alice.

"You're the one who lives next door to Bouncer's pet, right? In that place they call Earth. On Planet Hawick."

Dylan grinned.

"Other way around. For both planet and pet. Kind of."

"It's a 'yes', then?"

"Yes what?"

"The general wants to see you. Like right now."

"I'm not going without Alice."

"Take her with you," suggested Bouncer. "She's the one with the brains." Dylan's turn to frown until the girl stood up for him:

"Not true!" she said. "Dylan always comes top in everything at school. And why does the general wish to see him, I'd like to know?"

Perhaps sort of interested in what happens to me? the boy hoped.

"Council of War," replied the Doberman.

"Me too?" queried Bouncer.

"Of course, Captain."

The boy and girl looked to each other for help. Neither knew anything about war apart from what they'd seen in the latest Star Wars movie at the Tower Mill cinema. But Dylan was game for anything if it would help him outflank Colin McPhail in the one battle that truly mattered. Nevertheless, he wasn't sure a penknife and Alice's mum's dressmaking scissors would be of much use against the canine armies of Dogtopia. He badly needed a more effective weapon.

They followed Bouncer and the Doberman to the other side of the coal house where a dozen or more dogs of various breeds had gathered around a military mountain of dog, General Scratch. Dylan wondered whether the big barrel dangling from the general's neck really contained brandy, or whether it was merely a status symbol.

"Our spies tell me the rotts are planning a full-scale attack to wipe out all resistance to Bruiser's regime, but we don't know when and we don't know how," boomed the general.

"Do we know if Bosona's still alive?" asked George the corgi.

"That we do know. She is!" replied Scratch. "But when Great Dogover festivities are over in three days' time, unless we do something, she'll get thrown into the Bitch Ditch." Gasps of horror swept through the dogs as if this fact were the worst thing ever.

"What's the Bitch Ditch?" Dylan whispered into the ear of a Doberman standing beside him.

"Where he keeps females who displease him. Including bitches who refuse to bow to his authority. Or those he wishes to humiliate for whatever reason. A quick execution would be a more honourable death for our beloved leader. He gets palace humans to pelt them with scraps from the kitchen floor. Chewed bones... plus even worse stuff."

Dog poop? wondered Dylan. He feared for his sister. If the rottweilers were capable of such cruelty towards their own species, what might happen to ducks in Dogtopia?

"Do dogs eat ducks?" asked the boy.

The Doberman was about to say something when Alice nudged Dylan with her elbow.

"What?" he asked.

"Don't say things like that! It upsets me."

"Sorry!"

"Ducks? A great delicacy for rotts," the Doberman growled. "Special occasions only, though. Like the feast of Great Dogover."

Oh, my God! thought Dylan. *So soon!*

"We'll split into two groups," continued Scratch. "Attack on both sides before Bruiser mounts his offensive. I'll lead the first division through the forest and pick off any Wolf Police units we meet on the way. George and our new captain, Bouncer, will take the second division across the plain under cover of dark and hide in the poultry pens at the back of the palace on the far side."

"Excuse me, but are ducks considered poultry?" Dylan asked the Doberman. Alice nudged him again with her elbow.

"I heard that!" she said. "Please stop going on about ducks! It makes me feel so sad. And I keep thinking of Ben, too."

Dylan reckoned, *if I rescue Ben as well as Caitlin I might be in with a chance!*

"I'll find him. I promise," he promised.

"Don't make promises you can't keep!"

Alice was most definitely pouting. If she hadn't been so pretty, Dylan would have said it didn't suit her, but Alice being Alice, almost any expression she wore fascinated him. But now wasn't the time to stand and stare at the girl. Instead, he listened to the general:

"Captain Bouncer will take the two talking humans with him. He might be able to use them more effectively than I could. In fact, it has already been suggested to me that the male human should be made an honorary lieutenant." The St Bernard's plate-sized eye studied Dylan for a few unnerving moments. "Hmm. We'll see. But we do have an unexpected but pleasant surprise. A rott who has defected. Ron will also join Bouncer's division."

For a few moments, confusion reigned. The assembled dogs clearly did not know how to take this bit of news. Rotts were hated above all else. Their cruelty was almost beyond belief. How could a rott ever be trusted? But Ron, the general assured them, was different. He had saved Scratch's life when the rotts and wolves decimated the palace army. The general hushed the assembled dogs with a sweeping glance, then demanded they treat Ron not only as a trusted soldier but as a friend.

"After all," the general continued, "at the end of the day Ron is only dog! Now, any questions before we go our separate ways?"

Dylan had two: food and drink? He put up his hand.

"Food and drink?" he asked. "For humans, I mean."

"Human food and water? With the humans, of course! You'll have humans in your division. Most of our soldiers have pets, like Captain Bouncer." Dylan still had trouble coming to terms with the fact that Alice was a dog's pet.

"I have another question," he said.

When the huge St Bernard gazed down at him, the boy saw wisdom in those large, sad eyes.

"Yes?"

"Scissorman. Who is he? Which side is he on?"

No gasps from the other dogs this time. Only a deathly hush. But the general's eye did not falter. Slowly, the huge head nodded.

"Indeed! Scissorman!" was all he said, as if turning over an unanswerable question in his canine mind. "Well, my friends, our meeting is at a close. And may the Great Dog be with you all. Let us pray we meet up again, not in Dogeaven but in the Palace of Bosona!"

"Long live Bosona!" someone shouted. At which all dogs joined in with a tuneless chorus of 'Bosona Forever!' before dispersing.

"I'm so sorry," Dylan said when he saw Alice crying. All the dogs had left to prepare for uncertain destinies. Alice and Dylan were now on their own. He blamed their shared predicament on himself, but, without warning, the girl suddenly threw her arms around Dylan. That's when he decided he most definitely had a lot to learn about girls.

"No," she sobbed. "*I'm* sorry. For always being so mean to you. But I can't even begin to think of a life without my brother. It's nothing to do with you."

Nothing to do with me? To do with Colin instead? Houston, we still have a problem!

"I do care about Caitlin," Dylan informed her. He left out '...even though she can be annoying at times'. "That's why I want to know more about Scissorman. D'you think we'll see the professor again? Whatever they say about us humans, he has to be the brains behind the resistance here in Dogtopia."

"I'll ask Bouncer to find out what he can. From the corgi, maybe."

"George the corgi. Fatso, ay? Did you know the Queen has owned more than thirty corgis in her life?"

Alice giggled through her tears.

"How d'you know that?"

"Royal connections," he teased. In truth, he had surfed the dog internet one evening, frantically looking for dog facts that might impress the Chinese girl. Little did he think back then that he'd be attempting this in a dimension where human and dog roles were reversed. But the good news was that she did appear to be both amused and impressed.

"I wish I could be just a wee bit cleverer," the girl said. "Like you and Ben."

"I'm sure he loves you as you are," Dylan said. 'He', of course, also referring to himself. "We'll get your brother back. Even if I have to confront Scissorman myself. Come on! Better check out the food situation with those barking humans."

"Barking mad, ay?" She giggled again. A cue for Dylan to laugh at her joke.

"Yeah! Think I'd go mad if I just barked all day long."

They walked round to the front of the coal house where the dogs had already amassed into two divisions. Bouncer stood in the middle of his, talking with George. The human 'pets' sat on the ground in small groups, barking at each other. All had rucksacks. Dylan glanced at Alice.

"Are you thinking what I'm thinking about what's in those?" he asked. If only he'd known what was going to happen, before leaving the house that morning, he'd have filled his Superman rucksack with food raided from the fridge. As it was, he'd brought only one small packet of Sugar Puffs which he had already given to Alice.

"How are we gonna get them to share with us?" asked the girl. "I don't bark!"

Dylan walked over to the nearest human, a thin little woman whose rucksack looked way too heavy for her. He pointed to this, then showed her his own and gesticulated with his hands to imply she'd be better off with something lighter. She merely barked at him. Then another and another human joined in. The noise became deafening. Alice, meanwhile, ran off to seek out Bouncer. Moments later, the goldador bounded up to Dylan, Alice running behind him. To the boy's surprise, after the dog barked at the humans, their noise stopped. Rucksacks were opened, then grubby hands offered Dylan leather bottles, filled with water, and bits of food: strips of dried meat, sweet-smelling cakes and dried fruit. Dylan's Superman rucksack was soon near to bursting. Her neighbour wanted to release Whiskers to make more room, but Alice insisted they keep the mouse well-hidden. She couldn't bear the thought of the little creature ending up as a plaything for a hundred or more giant soldier dogs, so Whiskers got stuffed into a rucksack side pocket together with a handful of cake crumbs.

"Thanks for that, Bouncer," Dylan said. "But how come you can still bark?" If the dog had had human shoulders, he would have shrugged them.

"Didn't know I could till I gave it a go."

Dylan said he wondered about trying a little cambo juice himself in case this might enable him to both speak and bark.

"Don't you dare!" warned Alice, so he dropped the idea. But his other suggestion sounded cool to her. It involved him cutting a thin strip of elastic from the waist of his underpants (she flatly refused to offer her own underwear elastic), cut a bendy branch, which, with the elastic, he fashioned into a bow, then proceeded to make a dozen arrows. Alice cut the notches and fitted sharp heads of fragments from a smashed flint.

As Dylan was poking around, looking for feathers to serve as flights, George came bounding up to Bouncer. Rather, it was more of a fast waddle. Dylan had to suppress the giggles every time he saw the corgi attempt to move about quickly.

Do running pigs wobble like that too? he asked himself.

"He's here!" George said.

"Then we're ready!" responded Bouncer.

"Who's here?" asked Alice.

"Professor Pringle, of course!"

"Feathers?" Dylan asked George. "Any ideas? For these." He held up an arrow. "A lethal weapon. Could kill wolves and such like from far off, but they need feathers."

George sniffed the arrow and cocked his head.

"The poultry pens," he replied.

Caitlin? wondered Dylan.

***

Ben pulled his spear free from the dead wolf and wiped off the blood on the animal's fur.

"Can you take me to the palace, please?" he asked.

"It's where I'm going, chum. But how come you speak?" replied Ali. "I've not heard of a talking human apart from the professor. Unless—did those other dogs bring you? The ones they say the professor's gone to collect?"

"It's a bit of a long story."

"We've a long walk to the palace. Plenty of time for a long story."

So, as Ben and the Alsatian trailed along the edge of the forest, side by side, towards the hills that would lead them

78

to the mountain, the Chinese boy explained everything. How a goldador called Bouncer had been his sister's pet back in Hawick on Planet Earth, in another dimension, how desperately unhappy she was when Bouncer went missing—and how the boy next door had turned up, the evening before, with Bouncer's collar.

"Must be where the professor goes to, this place called Hawick. Do all dogs there really wear collars and bark?" enquired Ali. "Collars are pretty special here."

"All over Earth! Plus, people talk and dogs bark. Dogs with collars. And no one's heard of Dogtopia."

"But you said this boy's sister, called Caitlin, got turned into a red-haired duck and is being held captive in the palace here in Dogtopia."

"Because of Scissorman."

"Oh—bad news for poor Caitlin. And us!"

"What do you mean?"

"Ducks are a great delicacy. Particularly special ducks. And a red-haired one's sure to be special. Worth an absolute fortune in crystal. If Scissorman sells her to Bruiser, they'll keep her alive for the feast of Great Dogover, that's for sure. Afterwards Bosona gets thrown into the Bitch Ditch. And with all that crystal, Scissorman will become more powerful than ever before. That's *our* bad news!"

"Never mind crystal, Bitch Ditches or Bosona," said Ben. "I just have to get to Caitlin before Great Dog—... whatever."

"Great Dogover! And I do mind about Bosona. She's our leader, for Dog's sake!"

Ali sounded cross. Seeing the size of him, and remembering the mess he made of those wolves, Ben thought an apology was called for:

"I'm sorry. Didn't mean to be disrespectful. I just can't bear the thought of any harm coming to my little neighbour. It goes against being a doctor, see."

"Apology accepted. So long as we help each other. And you promise to be my pet. Which means I'll have to find you human food." Ben reckoned this part of the deal seemed a good idea. Having Ali on his side, too.

"Two days," the Alsatian said.

"What's two days?"

"Great Dogover. In two days. We must reach the palace by nightfall. Festivities start tonight. On the eve of Great Dogover, tomorrow, every dog will be pissed."

"You mentioned food." Ben, not having had any breakfast, was starving.

"The rebel camp's not far. Plenty of human food there. And you can lap water from the stream."

Ben had never 'lapped' water. If they had bamboo, like near his grandparents' place in China, he could have manufactured a straw.

They soon reached the rebel's camp. It was set in a secluded glade beside a fast-flowing stream. A group of humans had made a primitive shelter from broken-off fir branches, and sat in a circle, growling and barking. They stopped and stared when Ben and Ali approached. Each had a rucksack beside him or her. Fearful children clung to their parents. At the back of the shelter were sacks of what Ben took to be food. Human food. There were also several leather water bottles lying around, so Ben reckoned he wouldn't be needing a bamboo straw.

"This human saved my life!" Ali called out to the other dogs. "He killed a wolf with that stick. And he can talk like the professor."

The 'killing' bit wasn't strictly true. Earlier, Ben had felt certain he was about to be eaten alive by a mega-wolf, but he considered it would now be wise to stand still and let a dozen or so appreciative giant dogs sniff and lick him in turn. This was clearly the Dogtopian way of showing friendship. He dried his face on the sleeve of his jumper, glad to be without a tail. If he'd had one, they might have sniffed his bottom too, as he'd often seen Bouncer do with other dogs whenever he accompanied Alice and the goldador to Wilton Lodge Park in Hawick.

"My pet will need both food and a rucksack. In return, he can teach your humans to make things called spears. And show them how to use them against wolves."

It was clear to Ben that Ali was the leader of this pack of rebels. It felt good to be the boss's pet, for the other humans would look up to him as their leader. Using his sharpened flint, he spent a couple of hours helping them make spears. Even little ones for the children who quickly lost their fear of him. With hand gestures, he showed the humans how to turn their makeshift spears into weapons. He also tried simple speech, like "Me Ben, you—?" but they only barked. Nevertheless, they weren't stupid, and soon he was having productive conversations using a mix of grunts, sign language and body action. From the admiring way they stared at him, he began to feel he must truly be invincible. And he now had a personal army with which to rescue Caitlin. He preferred to think of the humans' relationship with Ali and the rebel dogs as more of an alliance than that of a bunch of pets obeying their masters.

Whilst training the humans, Ben overheard snippets of conversation between the dogs. Ali told the others how his new pet came from another dimension called Planet Earth where dogs bark and humans speak. A jumpy Chihuahua, small compared with its comrades, though still the size of a small Shetland pony, explained how he'd heard that the professor had built a machine that linked up with Earth and that he was planning to bring Earth dogs back to Dogtopia to rebuild General Scratch's army. Perhaps, Ben wondered, this might include Alice and Dylan. How he longed to know that his sister was all right.

When they set off, Ben had a rucksack full of enough dried food and bottles of water to last several days. But they didn't have several days. Only two before the feast of Great Dogover. Fortunately, the dogs were fast, lolloping along like trotting horses. Ben, fit from *tai chi*, jogged beside his owner as the other humans did with theirs. They encountered no resistance from wolves, and soon reached an undulating terrain where the forest merged with the hills. They continued to follow the stream, smaller and steeper and, in places, cascading over rocks, whilst Ben learned from his owner about another danger:

Rotts!

The rotts, Ali explained, were far worse than their wilder cousins, the wolves, for, being more intelligent, they could hunt alone. Wolves only functioned in 'packs' ("same word we use for groups of wolves back home on Earth," Ben said) which perhaps explained how easy it had been to overcome the two they'd encountered earlier on. "Mindless", Ali called them, whereas rotts were "cunning". Ben now feared for poor Caitlin even more should she be handed over to the rotts.

"No, they'll not touch her till Great Dogover Day," reassured Ali. "Any rott or wolf who played with such a special duck would get thrown into the Pit!" he added.

The Pit? Ben learned that whereas the 'Bitch Ditch' was the worst possible humiliation for a female dog, the Pit was the ultimate in punishment for any dog. Not only certain death, but also a slow and terrifying one.

"How come?" asked Ben.

"Cats," replied Ali, as if the very word explained everything.

The two rebel armies, dog and human, took rest concealed by a dense thicket at the foot of a hill on which few trees grew. Beyond that, a series of naked hills of increasing height, like stepping stones, led to Palace Mountain. Ben could see the palace more clearly. It was massive, its turrets punching the sky like angry, clenched fists.

"Built by humans long ago, some say," Ali remarked on seeing Ben gawping at the awesome edifice.

"What?"

"There's a legend that thousands of years back there were intelligent, talking humans in Dogtopia who built the palace for their masters. You'll have noticed that we dogs don't have hands like you lot. It's why we're always saying, 'a human is a dog's best friend'."

"Funny, but back home we say the same thing about dogs. Bouncer was a great friend for Alice."

"Your sister... does she have no human friends?"

"She's the most popular girl in her class at school. Caitlin's brother, Dylan, is a bit of loner, though. If Alice does come over with those Earth dogs, I hope it'll be with someone a bit less of a geek than him. Her latest boyfriend is an ace rugby player. He's called Colin."

"What's a geek?"

"Books and learning and stuff. Not that I can talk. But I am pretty clued-up on martial arts."

"Meaning?"

Ben laughed.

"Killing wolves and rotts with bare hands as well as spears. But what's with those cats in that Pit?"

"Don't you have cats on Earth?"

"Yeah! Bit more cute 'n' cuddly than dogs where I live in Hawick."

Ali laughed.

"Cats cute and cuddly? I like it! Almost half the height of those trees and with teeth as long as your spear."

"Um—different cats, I guess. How did they—?"

"Scissorman. A long while back. Before the Revolution and during the Reign of Terror."

"We had a Reign of Terror on Earth too, only it happened *after* a revolution."

"The pit bulls ruled back then. It's why they got called 'pit bulls'. Short for 'bullies', I guess. Scissorman gave them a pair of small cats. Kittens. No bigger than me. From Catalasia. To trade for crystal." Ben looked up at his owner and tried to imagine a horse-sized kitten. Not so cuddly, he had to agree.

"The cats bred in the Pit. Prefer their prey alive. Take pleasure in playing with it before devouring the poor dog limb by limb. There's a rumour that your head's still alive when it's the only thing left. Yuk, those cats! Of all the bad things Scissorman's done, bringing cats to Dogtopia was the very worst."

"Why does he do it?" asked Ben.

"Cats?"

"Cats, ducks—whatever. What's he get out of it?"

Ben had already learned that, on Earth, humans rarely do anything for nothing. It went against his father's Buddhist teaching, which was all about compassion and helping others, but it was a sad fact of life.

"Crystal power."

"Explain!"

"Don't you have crystal in Hawick?"

"Course we have crystals! Salt crystals, ice crystals, stuff in the science lab at school. And in the rocks around Hawick. They're volcanic, you see. Crystals are everywhere on Earth, but there's nothing special about them."

"Crystal is how he gets his magic. And it's kept in one of the palace towers. That's all I know. He'll probably get over a month's worth of magic out of that girl he turned into a duck."

"The man I saw didn't have a face. Just a sort of black space with red eyes."

"It comes and goes, they say. With his power. Not many outside the palace have seen Scissorman like you have, let alone his face. Which some say is worse than that of a cat. Could be that the crystal power he gets in exchange for the red-haired duck will give him a face like none other."

Ben swore, then, that he would kill Scissorman if it was the last thing he ever did. And if the monster had already handed Caitlin over to the rotts for their celebratory feast on Great Dogover Day, he would achieve this by throwing the man, magic or no magic, into that Pit to face gargantuan cats.

"Are you ready?" Ali shouted to his rebels.

"We are!" roared the assembled dog army.

"Remember, dog looks after dog! And respect your pets. With the teaching they've had from my human, Ben, they might save your lives as he did mine. Long live Bosona!" Cries of "Long live Bosona!" resounded, in the wooded hills, so loudly that Ben feared the rotts might hear the battle call in the palace up on the mountain. But common sense encouraged him to join in. Who- or whatever Bosona was, she couldn't offer anything worse than the fate awaiting Caitlin should their mission fail.

Chapter 6

Professor Pringle emerged from the coal house looking, as always, studiously confused. He peered at the two units of patiently-panting, blue-capped dogs and smiled.

At least something's right if he's smiling, thought Dylan.

He wanted to go up to the professor and ask whether he knew of any magical ways of turning red-haired ducks back into humans, but feared this might displease Alice.

A time and place for everything! Just before a life-changing battle in the alien dimension of Dogtopia was neither the time nor the place to upset his pretty neighbor. He felt a curious relief when the old man spotted him together with Alice and came over to them.

"I'm just so pleased you two survived the Vortex and have joined us in our struggle. And be sure of it, Bouncer will look after you. He so loves his pet."

So do I, thought Dylan, though didn't dare say it.

"I think we'll need better weapons than these," suggested Dylan, opening his rucksack and extracting the small penknife and scissors to show the professor. "Something special!"

"Special, huh?" The old fellow took them and turned each over a few times as if looking for anything that might identify them as worthy of being turned into 'special'. *Made in Sheffield,* perhaps?

"Just a penknife and scissors," observed the boy, his frown betraying anxiety. "Not much help against—"

"Wait here," interrupted Pringle. He disappeared back into the coal house with the two items and was gone for ages. Whilst the dogs continued to talk amongst themselves, Alice looked sad and Dylan kicked at the gravel in front of the building imagining he was kicking at rotts and wolves who were wanting to do bad things to his little sister. When the door finally opened, and the professor reappeared carrying a penknife the size of a machete and a pair of scissors that looked like a double-bladed sword, both Dylan and Alice gasped.

"Magic!" Alice exclaimed.

"No, my child," said the old man. "Science! It's what Scissorman uses. Crystal. Something rare and precious that we can use in this dimension and that I once came across on Earth. Somewhere in South America."

Dylan wondered whether the material might also give him muscles like Colin's, but to ask this in front of Alice would not have been sensible.

"But Scissorman uses his fingers to do stuff. That's got to be magic," Alice insisted.

"No, it isn't. And it'll be his downfall. He's as stupid as he's bad, I can assure you!"

"Those scissors of Alice's mum—" Dylan began to ask. "Can they now, um, you know... like Scissorman's fingers? Kind of do stuff that looks like magic. To us. Only here it's science. Transmogrification?" He was, of course, referring to Caitlin's transformation into a red-haired duck. He liked the word transmogrification and was proud to find a use for it in front of Alice, though sad about the reason for this.

"I told you, Dylan. Scissorman is stupid. But don't underestimate the power of his evil. Now, enough of this time wasting! Scottie's still seeking out more BUDS dogs back in the Scottish Borders. I'll come with you to the palace where we'll wait for reinforcements."

Dylan wished it was the Kelso Dog Show weekend. Every summer, they had a show in Springwood Park in the town of Kelso, with more shapes, colours and sizes of dogs than anyone could possibly dream of. If they were all to join the Bosona cause, General Scratch should have no difficulty overpowering the rotts. Still, with a bit of luck Scottie might yet come up with a bunch of border terriers, although the normal-sized ones Dylan had seen, when not in the company of his father, had always seemed docile. *They might behave differently if told to think of rotts and wolves as sheep substitutes*, he reckoned.

In the presence of his father, all dogs became aggressive. Dylan once wondered whether this was because of his dad's aftershave. It was powerful stuff and, as far as the boy was concerned, served no useful purpose. Indeed, like the man's limp, it offered Colin and his schoolmates yet another excuse to tease Dylan. Should he and Alice ever return to Earth, the first suggestion he would make to his dad, before again doing battle about becoming a vet, would be to leave off the aftershave. At least, on school days.

Thankfully, the professor, for whom Dylan's head was bursting with questions, was in their unit. Clearly, he was hugely respected by all the dogs, most of whom were Earth dogs who had as much difficulty as Dylan did in coming to terms with the idea of Pringle being the pet of a fellow canine, Bosona. For the time being, Dylan kept all questions hidden in his brain. Things had gone reasonably well on the Alice front, but he could not afford a wrong move by asking a question that might offend or make her tearful. If he had but known what the girl was truly capable of, questions would have bubbled out through his lips like the fizz from a shaken can of Irn Bru.

After Alice had slotted the scissors into the belt of her jeans, she had become, in his mind, a magnificent Asian Amazon warrior whilst he, with the giant penknife hanging from *his* belt, felt like a Caucasian Crusader from Robert the Bruce's army. The historical accuracy of such a military alliance was of no importance. Together they would depose the usurper, a rottweiler called Bruiser, find Ben and free Caitlin. How to turn his sister back into a human had been one of the questions to put to the professor, but for the time being it would remain inside his skull. No point in upsetting the 'Alice balance'.

General Scratch's unit set off first since the forest gave them daylight cover. Bouncer's unit, which included George, rested till sunset, building up their strength (and courage) for the sprint across the plain under cover of darkness. Bouncer sat lazily comparing his canine life in the Scottish Borders with the lives of his BUDS underdogs. From the cocked heads, drooping tongues and the panting of his listeners, it seemed that life had a lot going for dogs like him back in Hawick. Scrumptious food, plenty of bones to chew on, rubber toys to play with and, best of all, no rottweilers or pit bulls to worry about, though a few stories of dangerous dog encounters in parks were shared. But there was one dog who did not appear at all interested in the tales (or tails) of others. The fancy poodle bitch who wore her cap tilted to one side. However, she did seem to take undue interest in Dylan and Alice. The boy could not remember ever having seen her in Hawick. Perhaps she knew Alice from the park, he reckoned. Who wouldn't want to look at Alice?

Dylan seized the opportunity to find out more about Alice's past and her family in China:

"I'm *so* pleased I wasn't born there," the girl told him. "In the big cities, until recently, parents were only allowed one child. Just imagine having no brother." But the tears this generated in the girl troubled Dylan. He trawled his confused mind for a change of topic, and never let on how he had constantly fantasised about *not* having a little sister. Nevertheless, he did now desperately want Caitlin back.

"In China, what happened if another kid just arrived like? Unintended," he blurted. Alice blushed deep pink, so he changed the subject. "Um—do you eat with chopsticks back home?"

"A brilliant idea, Dylan!" she exclaimed.

Well there are lots more where that came from, he wanted to say, though didn't risk it. "How come?" he asked instead.

"No knives and forks here. Those barking people probably use their fingers. Not hygienic. Could you cut me four sticks from one of those trees, please?"

In response to the smile she gave him, he would have done anything. He ran to the edge of the forest, broke off a branch bearing straight twigs, and returned with a handful of sticks, grinning like a lottery winner. It was the first time that the Chinese girl had ever properly smiled at him. His confidence tree grew so big it would have filled the whole of Hawick—had he been in Hawick. Realisation that they were soon to battle against enormous wolves and rotts shrank it a little, but he still felt curiously happy as he handed the girl a bunch of sticks. She selected four of the correct thickness and length, then, with the aid of his magnified penknife, he stripped these free of bark for her and cut the ends to make them smooth.

"There you go," he said handing them back to Alice. "Two pairs of chopsticks. Now show me."

"What?" she asked.

"How to use them."

"Oh!"

After a short lesson, he became, in his opinion, an expert. In addition, he was taught to say "hello", "thank you" *and* "please" in Mandarin Chinese. Plus, he learned everything there was to be known about tea making, for Alice's grandparents lived in a village where tea production was the local industry.

"What?" he exclaimed in alarm. "They have a swallow's nest *inside* their house?"

"Brings good luck!" she informed him. But this was one fact he would certainly keep secret from his father. Dog poop in the street was one thing, but bird shit in the living room would have made the man apoplectic. He imagined his father, if told, foaming with fury. Dylan's Dad would even give a feather in a street wide birth. 'Bird flu' was his excuse.

Before setting off, Alice and Dylan ate with chopsticks and drank under the watchful gaze of Dogtopian humans. And the poodle. The girl fed a few crumbs to Whiskers, then carefully returned the mouse to Dylan's rucksack, this time safely wrapped in the boy's hankie, as well as Caitlin's dress, to keep it warm. Alice's idea.

"You really don't mind, do you?" she checked.

"Why should I? I'm gonna be a vet, aren't I?"

"Will you need an assistant?" she asked. "I'm good with animals."

Dylan could not believe his ears.

Please God, tell me I'm not dreaming! That was Dylan's silent prayer just before Bouncer's BUDS division set off, in the dark, at a canter, across the barren, open plain.

***

It was getting dark. Ali decided they should use the fading light to scale the hills and reach the poultry pens by nightfall. An intelligence scout, a long, boney whippet had been successful in recruiting mercenaries from another dimension, although the rebel leader remained unconvinced that alien dogs would be up to much when pitted against Dogtopian rotts and wolves. Nevertheless, General Scratch, albeit well past the task of command as far as Ali was concerned, had some sort of an army. His forces could provide a distraction whilst the rebel troops stormed the palace. He had every confidence that, with the backing of their armed pets, they could defeat Bruiser and reinstate Bosona as Top Dog. He had, of course, another motive, another plan, of which no other dog was aware.

Co-operation between the trained rebel forces and General Scratch's untrained rabble army was essential, so Ali left three dachshunds behind in a temporary billet hidden by a thicket. Stumpy legs made them cumbersome, so their fighting skills were limited, but their talking skills were second to none. Dieter, Dirk and Dora, the dachshunds, could fill the general in on detail and, if nothing else, might provide the professor's mercenaries with entertainment on the eve of battle. They could bring a house down with their uproarious 'sausage dance'.

Ben, having spent several hours making spears and teaching martial arts to the rebels' pets, was beginning to tire when they set off, so Ali suggested the boy scramble up onto his back for the strenuous climb over the hills to Palace Mountain.

Cavalry? Great idea!

It came to Ben in a flash. He'd seen countless historical movies in which cavalry had been the decisive factor in battle. After he mentioned this to Ali, all spear-bearing humans ended up on their owners' backs. The rebel army that snaked over the dusk-darkened hills was now truly a force to be reckoned with. There were several stops for water at the many streams that cut shallow valleys into the flanks of those hills. By the time they reached the foot of the mountain, night had engulfed the alien land.

The sentry kennel, beside a zigzag path that led up to the palace, was empty.

Why?

Ben could now see that Ali had been right to choose the forty-eight-hour lead-up to Great Dogover to mount his attack. It transpired that all guard dogs had been recalled to the palace for the celebrations. As far as the usurper Top Dog was concerned, this served a dual purpose. These dogs could pay homage to their new leader plus they would maintain order during the festivities when bonahol, a fermented bone drink, would be freely available. Opposition to Bruiser's rule would melt away under the influence of bonahol, but the downside would be the fights and skirmishes this invariably provoked. An augmented guard dog presence in the palace courtyard was therefore deemed essential. The Wolf Police alone could not be relied upon since most would quickly become legless after dipping their snouts into the bowls of bonahol scattered about. It was the duty of human servants to make sure these bowls remained full during the festivities which occupied the two days before Great Dogover.

The path ended on a high plateau more extensive than Ben had appreciated when viewing Palace Mountain from the plain. There were fields, a pond and, near the palace wall, several pens and huge outbuildings. A scattering of what looked like snow encircled the pond. Odd considering it didn't feel cold, even at the top of the mountain. Ben wondered whether the freezing point of water in this dimension was set at a higher temperature.

The boy slid off Ali's back and asked whether he could now search the pens for Caitlin.

"That red-haired duck?" queried Ali. Ben did not like the way the Alsatian licked a dog's equivalent of lips.

"She is *not* a duck! She's a human girl and I'm gonna change her back. Somehow! Or get Scissorman to do it. Before I kill him."

Ali laughed.

"I see I've found myself a brave pet! You might prove useful in battle. Yes, by all means see if you can find this *duuck* of yours." Ali seemed to hover over the word duck. *Can the Alsatian be trusted?* Ben wondered.

The humans, exhausted like Ben, sat huddled in whimpering groups outside the palace wall. Soon, they fell asleep. The dogs whispered amongst themselves for a short while before also succumbing to slumber. Even Ali, his large head on the ground, eyes closed, seemed dead to the world when Ben sneaked away to seek out Caitlin in the poultry pens.

***

There were a dozen empty pens, each attached to a vast shed the size of an airplane hangar. Contented clucking from within the nearest hangar informed Ben that the birds had been put to bed, but his heart sank when, after climbing over a wire fence, he entered the building. The stink of bird shit was suffocating, and the sheer number of hens, perched on low beams, staggering. Thousands, at a guess. To check every bird for a red-haired duck, and multiply this by twelve, would take all night. But he could see no other option, so, clutching his spear, he examined each sleeping hen one by one, carefully proceeding up and down the rows. An occasional fowl would open an eye, cock her head and offer a cluck or two, but none seemed unduly disturbed by the presence of a human. Perhaps, Ben reckoned, humans looked after the poultry whereas dogs ate them. It would be carnivorous dogs that these feathered creatures feared the most.

Ben moved on to the next shed—and the next and the next. Nothing but hens of varying colours and sizes. Not a single duck. He saw a few cockerels but stayed well clear of these. It must have been well past midnight when he left the last hangar shed in deep despair.

As he was making his way back to where the humans slept, he recalled a duck farm near his grandparents' home in China. The ducks were housed beside a duck pond. White ducks with orange bills, being fattened up for restaurants in Shanghai and Beijing where most would end up as 'Peking Duck' on the plates of wealthy, slavering clients. He had seen a large, wooden building at the far end of the pond. Where the shattered boy's burst of energy came from was a mystery, but he took off towards the pond like an Olympic sprinter.

The ground surrounding it was carpeted with white feathers, not snow. The door to the building was open.

Inside, thousands of ducks slept with their heads snuggled, eyes closed, on their backs. An occasional quack interrupted the silence. Caitlin wasn't a pure white duck. More of a white, green, blue and brown duck with, of course, a tufted crest of red human hair. Ben's heart sank when he saw, in the reflected moonlight, that the building housed only white ducks, but just before leaving he spotted a patch on the floor where duck droppings had been cleared away. Feathers, mostly white, but a few green and brown ones, had been carefully arranged to form letters:

CR PAL

CR PAL?

Clever little Caitlin had left behind a message: **C**aitlin **R**oss, **PAL**ace. She must have overheard talk about being transferred to the palace before someone, a human pet perhaps, grabbed her and carried her away. Not good news, but at least she was alive when they took her. He felt one step closer to saving his neighbour.

Although the boy returned with a heavy heart to where the humans slept, he now had both direction and purpose. The following day he would find Caitlin. With his hand still clasping the spear, he slipped into a deep and dreamless sleep.

***

Halfway across the plain, Alice showed signs of tiring. It was a long run. Even Dylan felt his muscles (sadly, not Colin-sized) begin to rebel. Alice stopped to catch her breath. Her neighbour called out to Bouncer:

"Hey, you're supposed to be looking after your pet! Can't you see she's tired?"

Alice scowled, too breathless to say anything. Bouncer bounded back to them.

"I am so sorry, Alice. I guess I'm just used to running on ahead of you at the park back in Hawick."

"Can't you give her a ride?" Dylan asked. "Like one of your lot is doing for the professor? She looks done in!"

"Why, of course! How silly of me. Should've thought. Up you get, Alice. Actually, there should be room for both of you."

And so, after helping Alice up, Dylan climbed onto the crouching dog's back behind her. Bouncer rose up and set off at a trot. At first the boy didn't know what to do with his dangling arms, but after the girl nearly fell off, he put them around her waist, clutching his hands together in front of her belly. And she made no objection. Sheer heaven!

Bet Colin's never done this, he thought. Or rather, hoped.

"Stay awake, Alice," he warned when the girl seemed to go floppy. She turned her head to face him, just inches away. Tears brimmed her eyes.

"I only did it to annoy you," she said quietly.

"Did what?" asked Dylan.

"Asked Colin home to see Bouncer. I was just so angry because of your dad. I wanted to get back at you. Before he shouted at me, I was going to ask you round to play with Bouncer and me, but I couldn't after what happened at the weekend."

"You were going to ask me round? I never knew."

"Well you know now!"

"Did he—I mean, you and Colin, did you—um?"

Dylan didn't know how to put the question that had been troubling him ever since spotting Alice and Colin together. The word 'kiss' seemed trapped behind his tongue. Alice looked away and Dylan feared the worst.

"Not that I know of," intervened Bouncer.

Alice turned to face Dylan again. Her tears now streamed so he decided to drop it.

"I honestly won't give up till we've found Ben and Caitlin," he promised.

"I know you won't," the girl said quietly.

It was already nightfall when Bouncer's division arrived at Palace Mountain. Alice and Dylan were advised to dismount at the foot of a scree. The dogs managed the climb more easily than the humans, and Dylan ended up carrying a small child as he clambered up the slope. Occasionally, he put the child down to offer a helping hand to Alice who stumbled about under the weight of her giant scissors... which he ended up carrying, as well as his mega-penknife, after handing the child to another human.

I may be a nerd with smaller muscles than Colin, but I bet he wouldn't act the gentleman for her like I do!

On this side of the mountain, a narrow ledge separated the palace wall from a sheer drop. No sensible dog would attack from the 'North Face', as George called it. Although Bouncer, the larger of the two dogs, was nominally in charge, George the corgi seemed to be the one making plans. Being a Dogtopian, he knew the terrain, but Dylan detected a growing tension between them.

"We should spend the rest of the night up against the wall here. We'll not be seen," suggested George. "Then, before first light—see that hole in the wall along there?" A shiny black corgi nose pointed at a double-decker-bus-sized opening in the wall out of which spilled heaps of the stinky brown stuff that Dylan's dad made such a song and dance about. Dog shit that Alice, in another dimension, always put into polythene bags if it came out of Bouncer.

"Yes! I see it." Bouncer was *not* wagging his tail. To wallow in sewage was not his idea of canine heroism. Besides, he knew that his pet hated uncleanliness of any description. No way was he going to force her into the palace sewer. "I hope you're not thinking of asking Alice to—" he began.

"It'll take us to the kitchen," interrupted George. "We'll soon overpower the human cooks up there. And their owners. Secure a base, infiltrate the whole of that level then locate the palace dungeon below. When Scratch gives the word, it'll be all out battle. Fighting throughout the palace. But with Bosona freed, I'm sure many of the palace guards will support her."

Bouncer looked unhappy. Alice sensed this but said nothing. From the girl's expression, Dylan could tell that she, too, was uneasy. After George had left, Bouncer turned from his pet, sank down onto his haunches, up against the wall, then stretched himself out in a pig-like canine repose. Alice beckoned to Dylan who had placed himself at a respectful distance from the girl. He cheerfully shuffled across on his bottom till their hips touched. His heart took off at a gallop.

"I'm not happy," she whispered. "And I know Bouncer isn't either."

"The battle tomorrow, eh?" enquired Dylan.

"Uh-huh! He's a totally non-aggressive dog. I don't know why he's been put up for captain."

"Can't see Porky Georgey getting much respect from the other dogs, can you? Have you seen how he wobbles when he tries to run?"

Alice giggled. He so loved to make her laugh.

Question is, does Colin also make her laugh?

"Yes, but that's not what worries me. There's something about that corgi," she said.

"Wants to show Bouncer up, perhaps? Make everyone know he's the brains in our unit?"

"Yeah, but—remember what Scratch said? About a traitor in our midst?"

"George? No way! Not sure about that shifty rottweiler, Ron, though. None of the other dogs talk to him. See him sitting over there all by himself at the far end of the wall?"

"Yeah! Bouncer can't stand rotts. Or pit bulls. Told me after we arrived. Oh Dylan, if only we could just find Ben and Caitlin and get out of this horrid place. I hate it so!"

"Remember, I promised we will! Just have to be—" Dylan rummaged through his brain cells for a word that might impress his classmate. "Vigilant! That's what it boils down to."

"Boils?" Alice's eyebrows approached each other in a curious frown.

"Well, not exactly boils. Figure of speech. Keep our eyes open. And absolutely no secrets. Between us, that is."

"Actually, you're not *that* bad," the girl said, grinning. Dylan's heart slowed, then sank, for he now feared she must have thought of him as totally worthless up till then.

What she means to say is, she would prefer it if I were Colin!

"The speaking bit, I mean," the girl explained. "In your letter, you said that you wrote it because you were no good at speaking and preferred to write things down. Well, I think you're pretty good with words. It's just that I'm so dumb!"

"You are not!"

"Yes, I am!"

"No, you're not!"

The conversation was rapidly descending to the level of pantomime assertion and denial, so Dylan suggested they should try to get some sleep. He positioned himself where, with one eye open, he could keep Ron within his sights all the time. Soon Alice was sound asleep. He saw the rott get up, peer around, sniff the air then disappear around the far corner of the palace wall. Crawling on his hands and knees, Dylan followed the dog. To uncover the traitor would surely go down well with the Chinese girl.

***

General Scratch was delighted to discover three rebel dachshunds hiding in a thicket at the edge of the forest where this merged with the plain and the hills. Apart from two savaged Wolf Police bodies, they had encountered no government forces. This disappointed the general. He'd hoped the EDDs would have had the chance to destroy a significant number of pro-Bruiser forest dogs. Some EDDs came with reputations of awesome ferocity—particularly those from Hawick. But when Dieter the Dachshund informed him that a strong rebel force would be gathered at the back of the palace, near the poultry pens, he felt encouraged. Their leader was an Alsatian called Ali, a dog he'd not come across in military circles, but whom, according to Dieter, the Wolf Police greatly feared.

"Plus, the rebels have got a talking human," Dora piped up. "Ali's taken him on as a pet. He used a spear to kill wolves with."

"A talking human, ay?" The general studied the dachshund for a few moments. "Did *your* human say anything about *our* two talkers?"

"You've got talking humans as well?"

"A young male and a bitch. In the second division. Led by an EDD captain. Bouncer."

"Pure coincidence!" remarked Dirk.

"No such word in military language! I wish I'd known before."

"About Ben? Why?" asked Dora.

"Never you mind, you inquisitive sausage! But does '*he*' know, I wonder?" Meaning, of course, Scissorman. To mention the monster's name at such a time could bring bad luck.

Dora, piqued at being called a sausage, waddled off muttering to herself.

"Excuse our sister," said Dirk. "Never was one for manners."

"You three can team up with the Scotties over there. And warn your sister that we're a proper military force, not a bunch of canine layabouts. Either she obeys orders or she's on her own. You two as well. Got it?"

"Aye, sir!"

Dieter and Dirk scampered off to pacify their sister whilst the general made a last-minute inspection of troops before setting off over the hills for Palace Mountain. To the humans, he looked like a mountain on the move himself.

Being led by a squadron of bloodhounds, the scent of the rebel army was easy for Scratch's division to pick up and to follow the trail. When they reached the foot of Palace Mountain, the scent was so overwhelming for the hounds that the general knew they must be hot on the heels of Ali's forces. Desperate to meet up with this mysterious Alsatian, he changed his plan. Instead of camping in a shallow valley near the summit of the highest of the hills, he chose to march on and overnight with the rebels. After all, there was now no risk of rear attack from the forest wolves, for there weren't any around. Bouncer, according to George's brilliant plan, would enter via the sewers whilst he and the rebels could storm the palace gates, when these were opened, to allow Bruiser's guards to carry out their daily dawn inspection of the palace perimeter.

The general was also eager to meet Ben the human and find out if there was any connection with Bouncer's pet.

***

Approaching the corner of the palace, Dylan struggled briefly with the dilemma of whether to let Alice, now fast asleep, out of his sight for a few moments, or earn her admiration by tracking the traitor, Ron the Rott. Bow in hand, he chose the latter and crawled into a smell from hell.

Another thing his dog-phobic dad went on about was 'dog smell'. This, apparently, was less to do with what they deposited in the streets of Hawick and more about the odours that emerged from panting canine mouths, and the bacteria that created these. Dylan had to admit to himself, but not to his father, that he was occasionally tempted to pinch his nose in the presence of old dogs, though always refrained from doing so. He saw it as bad veterinary training. But this was different. The smell trailing Ron the Rott came close to being a lethal weapon. It made Dylan feel dizzy.

I hope Alice will know I'm doing this for her, he thought as the aroma began to break down his brain's defences. He felt swimmy and sick whilst edging forwards, a few mouse-tail-lengths away from a one-thousand-foot drop, towards the far corner of the building.

104

How about inventing a mouthwash for dogs? Bound to impress her. Must ask the professor what he thinks. Could earn me a few quid. Buy a present for her.

Nearing the corner, Dylan observed that the steep cliff edge ended a few yards ahead where the path opened out. Beyond the palace were fields, buildings and dogs. Hundreds of them. Dylan watched as Ron trotted towards these. One, then another and soon a large number, stood up to face the intruder. A big Alsatian lowered his head and bared his fangs whilst uttering a threatening growl. This was the first time that Dylan had heard a Dogtopian dog growl like an Earth dog. Ron halted.

"I'm with General Scratch," he shouted. "Long live Bosona!"

The Alsatian raised his head and sniffed the air.

"Prove it," he replied.

Ron laughed.

"Give me one of Bruiser's wolves and I'll tear him apart for you! I'm with the second division of Scratch's BUDS Army."

"You're from that Earth place? Another reason not to trust you!"

"No. I defected from Bruiser's Forces. Intelligence, they call me."

"An intelligent rott? Almost as weird as a talking human." For a few moments, Dylan expected the sort of skirmish he'd once seen between two rival dogs in Wilton House Park, but the Alsatian chuckled then wagged his tail. "Ali, leader of the rebel army. And speaking of talking humans, I have one as a pet."

The two dogs approached each other and touched noses. Dylan reckoned Ali must be extremely brave to get so close to that smell. Even braver when he walked around Ron the Rott to sniff his 'bot'.

A 'talking human'? Could it be Ben?

"We've two, as well," offered Ron whilst being inspected by Ali. "A young male and a bitch. Only she's called a 'girl', whatever that means. The professor sent them here."

"Because of Ben, we've now got a whole human rebel force as well. Our pets are armed with weapons called spears. Ben killed a wolf with his. Not exactly teeth, but they can wound or even kill from a distance."

Ben-the-boy, not Ben-the-mongrel?

Dylan forgot the smell, the sheer drop and fact that he was sure to die in this alien land of dogs. On hearing the name 'Ben', he felt transported to heaven. Or Dogeaven?

Or how about Devon?

He and Caitlin were taken there on holiday with the family before she started to get on his nerves. It truly had been a holiday in heaven. He even enjoyed playing cricket on the beach with his dad. It must have been the last time they'd played together, and he remembered taking the runs slowly because of his father's limp.

But Ben here, in Dogtopia? Should he crawl back to wake up Alice and tell her, or first check out the veracity of this information? His brain imagined her pushing him over the precipice if it turned out to be a different Ben, so he followed the Alsatian, and the rott, at a safe distance.

Clearly, the rebel army had not picked up on Dylan's scent. Not surprising when Ron the Rott's odour still hung heavy in the air. The ledge narrowed to a thin strip of level ground. The boy stood with his back to the palace wall and side-stepped towards where the path opened out and where the rebel forces were camped.

The presence of Ron had caused a great stir. Dogs crowded around the rottweiler, plying him with questions, and all, to a dog, wagging their tails. To have a rott on their side was obviously a boost to morale. Dylan spotted a sprawl of sleeping humans in brown tunics close to a cluster of buildings which, from a distance, looked like aircraft hangars, yet couldn't be. Not even in Disney cartoons did dogs fly airplanes. He wished he'd brought his binoculars, for scanning the slumbering bodies he saw no Chinese boys. He did, however, spy a pair of jeans draped over a bush near a lake. The ground around the lake was sprinkled with snow, yet it seemed too warm for this.

Jeans... Ben? Snow... too warm... white feathers? Ducks... Caitlin?

Now Ben was so easy to pick out that Dylan could not believe he had missed him. The only human with short hair, and the only un-bearded adult male, he lay asleep surrounded by twenty or more Dogtopian pets. The talking dogs were so excited about the new arrival, Ron the Rott, that they failed to notice the Earth boy slip past towards the lake. A cow-sized ball of orange fluff, which if shrunk to normal size would have passed for a chow-chow, pointed two ears at him and opened one eye without lifting its head.

"I'm only a pet," Dylan whispered to the dog. The chow-chow seemed happy with this and closed its eye. The boy stepped over sleeping humans—men, women and children—to reach Ben.

His neighbour lay curled up beside a spear. As Ali had said, the humans had spears and here was Ben surrounded by some of his troops. In all, together with other groups spread out on the ground between the palace and hangars, there must have been well over a hundred humans.

"Ben!" whispered Dylan, shaking the older boy. Ben, grabbing his spear, scrambled to his feet. For a few seconds, they simply stared at each other. Then Dylan smiled at his neighbour.

"Dylan? What on earth are you doing here?"

"I could ask you the same question. Last time I saw you, you just disappeared through that open doorway in Number Twenty-four."

"It was awful. I mean, seeing your sister getting turned into a duck then vanishing into—" Ben paused, as if trying to work out in his head exactly what it was that he stepped into.

"The Interim?" offered Dylan.

Ben frowned. He slipped on his jeans.

"Is that what it's called?"

"It's what the professor said. You're lucky. Could've ended up in Duckdom. Or a place full of dinosaurs. Like I saw in the Vortex."

"The what?"

"Vortex. The professor's invention. Can help you travel across different dimensions. We nearly didn't make it because of a mouse called Whiskers."

"We?"

Ben's keen gaze nearly cut Dylan in half. How could he tell the Chinese boy that his young sister was asleep on a ledge beside the palace with a pack of dogs and bunch of barking humans?

"Um—Alice! And me... of course."

"What about Alice? I hope she's been a sensible girl and gone back home."

"Um—asleep. But not in her bed." Ben's eyes told Dylan he could no longer lie. "Round—um—there." He pointed to where he'd come from. "With a load of dogs and—um—humans. Barking humans, like."

Ben hung his head in shame. "What have I done?" he asked.

"A pretty brave thing. How were you to know there was no floor beyond that door in Number Twenty-four."

"The number one rule in martial arts, Dad always says, is to make no move until you're certain. But to see poor Caitlin taken away, all alone. I guess—"

"Guess you're just cut out to be a doctor. To help people. Anyway, Alice is gonna be over the moon to know you're safe."

"Not sure that's the right word, Dylan. Alive, yes. But safe? Who knows? God, if any harm comes to Alice, I'll... I'll—"

"You'll blame me, right?"

Ben laughed and gave his neighbour a playful punch in the ribs.

"Look, it seems we're gonna have to go along with this 'Save Bosona' thing if you're to get Caitlin back," he said.

"Plus keep in with the professor. This stuff called crystal might be the answer to Scissorman's magic."

"Oh man, those red eyes! Poor wee Caitlin! We've gotta rescue her. But look—" He reached into his pocket and pulled out Caitlin's good luck Chinese brooch. "I'm certain this helped me get here in that Interim place you mentioned. And somehow it's led me to the duck pond."

"Led you to the duck pond?"

"Well—to that huge building beside the pond."

Dylan looked across at the duck hangar.

"It's not snow, then. Like I guessed it wasn't."

"No. White feathers. And your brilliant sister left a message on the ground. Using some of her own feathers to give me a clue. CR PAL. Caitlin Ross, PALace. What a clever girl she is. They must've taken her to the palace before she could finish the word."

"In exchange for crystal, perhaps. Plus Bruiser plans to eat her as a special treat for Great Dogover. Then throw Bosona into the Bitch Ditch."

"Neither of which can we allow!" insisted Ben. "Look, these humans aren't as daft as they look. For the time being, I've gotta play the role of Ali's pet. I saw what he did to a couple of muckle wolves. But I'm not sure about him."

"I'm sure about General Scratch, but he is a bit old. A St Bernard, mind you. Huge but not that agile. Doubt whether he could jump through a flaming hoop like those police dogs at the Edinburgh Tattoo. But he's no daftie. He has his suspicions."

"About?

"A traitor in our midst. I'm sure it's Ron. The stinky rottweiler I followed round the side of the palace. He's over there, talking to an Alsatian called Ali."

"My owner. But what about Alice? You left her all by herself?"

In a flash, Dylan saw how stupid he'd been. Gripped by a desire to impress the girl he had left her in danger. What if Ron wasn't the traitor after all? He blushed crimson and felt something pulse in his chest, like his heart was beating at him from inside for putting at risk the life of the only girl he truly fancied. Ben, thankfully, smiled.

"I know how you feel about Alice," he said. "She's a great girl, and really, Colin is not a suitable boyfriend. I told her that. Apart from being able to pick up a rugby ball and run with it, there's not much else that dude can do. I was so pleased when you showed up again last night. Go back to her, tell her big brother's fine and we'll meet up in the palace."

Dylan's turn to chuckle.

"Guess what?" he said. Ben shrugged his shoulders. "Your sister is now the pet of her dog, Bouncer. Plus, *he's* the captain of our BUDS division. Bosona's Ultimate Dog Squad. Bit different from a doggy stroll in Wilton House Park, ay? At least, in one way, Alice and I are now 'buddies'."

Ben, too, chuckled.

"I ken. Look after her, mate. If anything happens to my sister, I'll hold you responsible. Okay?"

"And you'd better get mine back—human and unharmed!"

The boys high-fived. Dylan told Ben how he planned to collect some sharp flints and feathers, from around the duck pond, for Alice to fashion into arrowheads and flights. He held up his bow with its underpants bowstring elastic. Ben laughed and remarked that Colin would most definitely not have thought that one up.

"In the palace, then? With Alice?" said Ben.

Dylan nodded.

"And long live Bosona! Get some shut eye now, Ben. We'll all need our wits about us tomorrow."

Dylan stood up and left Ben to sleep on. He sauntered off to gather up handfuls of feathers and several sharp flints. As he stuffed these into his rucksack, together with remnants of poultry food for Whiskers (*does my sister have to eat this yukky stuff?*), a bloodcurdling howl filled the dark sky with fear. It came from behind the hen hangars. In the moonlight, a pair of large white almond shapes shone at him, then another and another, until he was half-surrounded by a crescent of giant wolf eyes.

All Dylan could think about was Alice's safety. With his bow slung over his shoulder, he backed away from the wolves. In the silence, the eyes shifted. Some to the left, others to the right, whilst one pair, which belonged to a head larger than the rest, moved forwards. Towards him. In Dylan's book, wolves were far from stupid, but they were pack animals. He had once read about animal psychology and the collective intelligence of a pack, partly to impress Alice should the opportunity ever arise. Anyone with more than a basic education (which excluded Colin) knew that the teamwork of a pack of wolves was a miracle of nature far greater than that of a rugby fifteen. He, Dylan Ross, would have to use his human brain to survive this wolf attack. Only if he were to survive would he be able to protect Alice. The large wolf coming straight for him was providing the trap he had to avoid. Slowed down, and perhaps disabled by a bite from that beast, the others, outflanking him, would make escape impossible. He was dead meat, unless...

The boy from Hawick ran to the palace wall, drawing his magnified penknife-come-sword. This, he held like a two-handed Scottish claymore. With his back to the wall he could not be surrounded, and his weapon was, he reckoned, even more deadly than wolf teeth.

As his mind darted from wolf to Caitlin to Alice, he vowed to kill Ron. Here was evidence that the rott defector was a traitor. How could the general have been so stupid as to trust that champion of halitosis? Why had they not been warned?

Chapter 7

"Dylan?"

Getting no reply, Alice sat up and peered at snoring humans a few yards away. She crawled to the edge of the cliff, fearful that the boy from next door might have rolled over the precipice in his sleep. Nothing as far as she could see, but it was a sheer drop that disappeared into the gloom of the night. Then she **realised**, with relief, that his ridiculous Superman rucksack was also missing. He had definitely taken it off before going to sleep. Probably, he needed to go to the toilet and had taken the rucksack to protect Whiskers from the dogs. How thoughtful of him. She was beginning to really like the son of her hated maths teacher.

The girl saw that Bouncer was awake and wished to warn him about George. Somehow, she felt certain that George was that traitor. Being a goldador, Bouncer was so good-natured that he would not harbour suspicions about anyone or anything.

She stood up and almost fell over. Before being able to walk, she had to shake out the pins and needles from her feet. The hard ground must have pressed on various nerves and things that Clever-Dick Dylan Ross was bound to know the names of. Oh, why couldn't she get good grades like him? It wasn't that she didn't try—certainly a lot harder than Ben who always got top grades and impressed his teachers despite spending precious little time over homework. It simply wasn't fair!

No, I mustn't have it in for Dylan for being brainy! I never blamed Ben for being that way. Anyway, I could do worse than have a boyfriend who wants to be a vet. At least until the day I get swept off my feet. A vet's assistant? Perhaps liking animals is the only qualification you need. Whatever, I honestly don't fancy being a supermarket checkout girl. My maths would let me down.

Just as feeling was returning to her feet, Alice noticed two white lights hovering above the path at the corner of the palace wall. Candles? Wrong shape. Horizontal instead of vertical. And they moved in unison. Then another pair appeared. She blinked a few times until the reason for the lights became clear. Two great wolf-shaped heads studied her from close to the ground, their almond-shaped eyes reflecting the hazy moonlight. A third pair appeared, higher up. This wolf, larger, was standing. Alice, unable to see Dylan anywhere, panicked. She ran to wake up Bouncer.

Her owner, already awake, must have smelt the wolves even before she spotted them.

"What do we do?" the girl asked. "And where's Dylan got to?"

"Just wake everyone up," Bouncer said. "Get the humans away from here. Into the sewer. Protect the children. With your—" He tapped at her scissors with a paw. "With this! And just forget about that stupid boy you call Dylan."

Alice, upset by this remark, winced.

"Where's the professor?" she asked. "He could perhaps use his magic. He may be old and frail, but I bet he's the only one who can get us both home." She was referring to herself and Dylan.

"I am *not* returning to that place you call home! My home is here!" Alice had already sensed a sea change in her relationship with Bouncer. Now was not the time to insist that she and Dylan return to Hawick. At least, not until Ben and Caitlin had been found. "The professor's over there with George. Oh dear—where's George gone?" questioned her pet.

The professor was snoring away, his head resting comfortably on the soft belly of a chow chow. But there was no George.

"I couldn't bear it if they've eaten Dylan," Alice said, blinking at the paired wolf eye-lights fixed on her.

"His comeuppance for having a father like Mr Ross if they have," suggested Bouncer. "I know how you really feel about that boy and your maths teacher. Glad to be rid of him, ay?"

"Stop it, Bouncer! Dylan's not like that! I must—"

"You, my little pet, must do as I say! Get these humans out of harm's way. At once! We'll meet up in the kitchen at the top of the sewer chute. When I and my division have done with those wolves."

Bouncer showed his teeth. This wasn't the friendly goldador she'd cared for since he was a bouncy puppy. Nor was it the time to tell her owner about her suspicions concerning George who, like Dylan, had vanished.

As ordered to, the girl awakened the humans and ushered them into the gaping, black sewer entrance. Her sneakers were soon caked in excrement and sticky bits of waste food. Fastidious though she was about cleanliness, there was nothing she could do about it. Holding the giant scissors in front of her with both hands, ready to snip at anything unpleasant that might show its face, she was unable to cover her nose. Inside the sewer, the smell was so overpowering that she began to feel sick.

A burst of canine fury erupted outside where, moments

earlier, she had been fast asleep dreaming about being back at school in Hawick. Dreaming about sitting next to Dylan and ignoring Colin when he talked to her. Now she had neither Colin nor Dylan to help her. The shouts and screams, snarls and growls, out there on that ledge, were unlike anything she'd heard before. Still unused to the voice of the dog who was once her pet, she had no idea which of the shouts belonged to Bouncer and which to the hundreds of other dogs and wolves locked in battle. The noise got closer, and the girl waved her scissors at the humans to drive them further up the sewer.

"Shoo!" she shouted. "Keep away from the wolves. Hurry on up into the palace! Woof woof!"

The humans barked back at her. Getting the message, they turned and, stepping over rubbish and dog shit, proceeded further into the tunnel. Alice spotted a narrow, raised ledge without excrement and, after some persuasion, with miming, encouraged the children to run along this rather than wade through sewage. She followed in the rear, turning frequently to make sure no wolves were creeping up on them from behind. They soon reached a chute littered with food waste. From the kitchen, perhaps? The other humans huddled at the foot of this, looking pleadingly at the Earth girl for instructions. Her cue to take the lead. On all fours, she scrambled up the steep slope. Only then would the others follow.

As Alice approached an opening at the top, voices became audible. Here, in Dogtopia, voices meant dogs. Cautious, she kept her head low, her nose horribly close to the putrefying contents of the chute as she peered into a large room.

Evidently this was the palace kitchen. Huge dog bowls,

some laden with questionable food, were dotted about. More importantly, George stood at the far end, talking to another corgi. Slightly smaller and less plump than George, this one also had black markings. George spotted Alice and came waddling over to her without wagging his tail. The girl tightened her grip on the scissors.

"Where's your owner? And why are you here so soon?" he asked. Alice wished to ask the same question of the corgi. The dog with black markings stood still, sniffing the air.

One of Bruiser's or one of Bosona's? The girl had no idea.

"A battle," she said. "With wolves. Bouncer said we were to meet up here."

"Gotta earn his collar somehow, I guess, being an Earth dog," muttered George. She backed away when he came closer. "There's more than just you here. I can smell. Are the other humans also armed?" he asked. Alice nodded. If George was the traitor, he would not attack her knowing that she had the backing of a hundred or so armed humans. "Tell them to come out of the sewer! And please try to bark properly! Tell them in bark-speak that they'll be quite safe here in the kitchen. It's all part of my plan. This is Carol, by the way. She's the kitchen maid."

Calling a dog Carol was one thing, but calling a dog called Carol a kitchen maid seemed totally weird to Alice.

"Carol, this is one of our talking humans from Earth. She can't even bark properly! You'll get used to them, though. The professor thinks they might help Bosona's cause."

Alice climbed out into the kitchen, ashamed of the odour that accompanied her.

"Woof, woof," she said to the other humans. George

laughed. One by one, they timidly emerged from the hole in the wall. Although the kitchen was big, it was barely adequate for the number of Dogtopian humans that spilled out. The children, clutching makeshift spears, looked terrified. Some whimpered like puppies.

"What is Bouncer playing at sending humanlings into the palace without dog guards?"

Humanlings? Is that what they call children here?

For some reason, this angered Alice. *'Dogling'* was the sort of word Mr Ross might have come up with for a puppy. How she hated that man! And to think he was Dylan's father. No way could she ever allow herself to be called the boy's 'girlfriend'.

"Like I was trying to tell you," responded Alice, "we were attacked. A big battle's going on out there. I'm really worried about Bouncer. And about all the other Earth dogs. They're not used to fighting horse-sized wolves. They certainly couldn't spare any guards for us lot. And why are you—?" She paused. Although outnumbered, George still had big canine teeth. "Um, what I mean to say is—"

"Why am I not out there with Bouncer? To tell the truth, we need to keep the brains alive and I, my little human female, am the brains of this outfit. Being made Captain is only a lure for dumb dogs like Bouncer. And now he'll be trying to earn himself a collar."

Alice bristled to hear Bouncer described as dumb. Traitor or not, she truly disliked George. She thought about Bouncer's red collar back home. This reminded her of Dylan, and it angered her that the boy had left her alone without saying where he was going. Even to know he was looking for a toilet (he did drink rather a lot of water) would have dulled the worry gnawing away at her insides. *But why should Bouncer need another collar here in Dogtopia?* She put this question to George.

"Dogs who show extreme bravery in battle get decorated with the Collar of the Top Dog. I've got two."

A fact that necessitated some self-control on Alice's part to suppress a giggle, for the plump corgi was not her idea of an award-winning fighter. Then, instead of giggles came sadness on recalling how Dylan likened George to a plump pig. Dylan always made her want to laugh. Colin only made himself laugh. Perhaps the boy next door wasn't so bad after all.

The muffled sound of voices emanating from the sewers came as a relief. It didn't sound like guttural wolf-speak.

"Your guards," reassured George. "Bouncer might yet get collared."

Moments later, the twins, Bill and Ben, bloodied, burst into the kitchen. Some of the humans whimpered and backed away from the mongrels, unsure.

"It was tough out there," said Bill, "but Bouncer's kind of got things under control. That's some owner you've got, Alice. There are bits of wolf all over the place. He soon worked it out. 'Break up their formation,' he ordered. The Wolf Police work as a group, see. They just don't know what to do when they're on their own."

"*I* told him that!" George seemed eager to make sure everyone knew he was the brains, not the goldador from Earth. "Does he want the human pets back with him, for what they're worth?" Alice, angered to hear her species so casually dismissed, was tempted to tell George that her scissors had magical properties, but on seeing the size of his teeth decided to stay quiet.

"No," replied Ben. "He's still checking the palace perimeter. Sweeping up wolf resistance. He'll join us here when he's ready. You should maintain control of the kitchen level whilst he takes a special action unit down to the dungeons. To release Bosona before they start preparing her for the Bitch Ditch."

"Got it all worked out, has he? Then ask your doggy master how he plans to take on the Doberman jailer."

"Doberman?" questioned Alice. The one she'd seen at the Kelso Dog Show was vast, even for an Earth dog.

"Dungeon Dobie. Nothing gets past that beast."

"Bouncer plans to take you, his pet, with him. He said you can lead the attack with your scissors," Ben told the girl.

So, Bouncer's still a big softie after all? thought Alice. But she said nothing. All she wanted was to meet up with Dylan again. Then the two of them could seek out the other Ben, her brother, rescue Caitlin the duck and plan their escape.

Soon, Professor Pringle emerged from the sewer, together with the chow chow he had been using as a large cushion.

"Thank goodness you're all right, my child. You must be exhausted."

"Do you know where Dylan is?" the girl asked. "He's vanished."

"Vanished? Surely not—unless he's ended up in the Interim. Oh, please don't worry about him, my dear. That boy's strong in self-preservation. As well as clever. Like you. It's why I chose you both."

"*You* chose *us*? I thought it was Bouncer you wanted."

"Oh—Bouncer. Hmm!" That wise old face gave away a lot more than the few words the man spoke. Alice puzzled over the look in his kindly eyes. She recalled her pet-turned-owner snapping at her. There again, what awful pressure there must be now for Bouncer, she thought. Plus, there was also George to contend with.

George the traitor?

"George thinks we shouldn't take on Dobie the Doberman," she told the professor.

"Quite right. That creature's for none other than Scratch himself. Why?"

"Bouncer decided he and I should attack the jailer with his special action unit."

"Hmm. I can also see *his* point. Secure the lower part of the palace whilst the General storms the main gate. Bosona will still have lots of supporters inside, of course. Those who kept quiet and weren't thrown to the cats in the Pit."

"But they'll get torn apart one by one by Dobie," warned George. "Dogs can only enter the dungeon singly. Dobie sleeps across the entrance, blocking it completely. He's grown so big he couldn't squeeze out of the place, anyway. They feed him constantly. With prisoners. It'd be suicide to take him on, if you ask me. Murder, even. Suicide for Bouncer plus he'd be murdering the others in his unit. Including his human pet. You!"

Alice felt uncomfortable. Being torn apart by a dog the size of a camel wasn't part of her game plan. Whilst she stood turning George's comments over in her mind, the elegant poodle bitch, whom Dylan had earlier pointed out, emerged from the sewer. She looked from George to Alice and back.

"Bouncer's pet is filthy!" she exclaimed in a refined, high-pitched voice. "The other humans, too. Even the professor. Get them cleaned up!" The way Poppy the Poodle approached Alice reminded the girl of a model strutting a catwalk. Her polished black nose sniffed at Alice's splattered jeans. "These things covering her legs. Wash them!"

For a few moments, George, the General's brains, stared in disbelief at the bitch. Poppy towered above him. Should he be taking orders from this prim Earth dog, he seemed to be wondering?

Alice, on the contrary, welcomed any suggestion of getting cleaned up. Although eager to be rejoined with Dylan, she did not wish for him to see her with sewage filth stuck to her trainers and caking her jeans. She unfastened these and slipped them down. She felt herself go hot and red in the face as male Dogtopian humans watched with interest. Poppy growled at them, and Alice liked the poodle even more for that. Standing in her panties in front of those bearded, barking goons felt awful.

Two female humans filled a bowl with warm water.

"Clean the human girl's shoes and jeans," commanded Poppy.

Whilst other female humans washed her feet and legs in the bowl, Alice's jeans and trainers were cleaned by the two helpers. That's when the Chinese girl from Hawick realised for the first time that Dogtopian humans were barefooted. Her trainers captured the women's interest for they smiled and barked at each other as they turned them over, looking for bits of dirt that might have been missed.

How odd I must seem to them, thought Alice. Then something totally weird happened. When one of the women held up her jeans, checking for spots of dirt, the poodle crouched down and wafted warm breath over them.

Hey, that's so cool! Poppy's like a giant hairdryer! I

must tell Dylan.

Alice giggled when the poodle-hairdryer was used to dry her arms and the rest of her body. Then, whilst pulling on warm, dry jeans, she asked Poppy if she knew where Dylan was.

"Slipped away!" was the dog's answer. "Coward, ay? Typical male." Alice did not believe that. Nerd, maybe, but coward, no!

More noise from the sewer. Voices. Bouncer's large head appeared.

"Safe, I see," he said to his pet. "Has Poppy been looking after you properly? I sent her on ahead of me." Alice glanced up at the poodle, grinned and nodded.

"Where's Dylan?" she asked again of her owner. She needed an answer.

"If I knew, he'd be here. If he's deserted, he'll pay the price."

Pay the price? Alice frowned.

The goldador stepped into the kitchen, followed by several other battle-scarred dogs. His select 'special' few to take on the Doberman? Perhaps George was right. Had they been smaller, and back in Hawick, these dogs could have passed for a bunch of timid pooches from an animal rescue pound.

"So, George, why weren't you out there fighting the Wolf Police like the rest of us? Even Poppy here showed her teeth." If dogs could wince, Alice was sure the poodle did just that. But George was not to be belittled:

"And how did you expect to ensure the safety of your pet if a dog with brains hadn't first cleansed the kitchen of enemy forces?" enquired the corgi.

Bouncer merely gaped, his large tongue hanging limp

from his blood-stained jaw as his gaze encircled the kitchen. Alice, for the first time, saw a khaki mound at the far end of the room, beyond the cowering humans.

"Go, boy," George said to one of these. "Show him."

A lanky male with red hair and a goatee beard ran to the mound and pulled back a canvas cover to reveal three corpses: three dead wolves, each with its neck ripped open.

"Carol and me," explained George. "Mostly me. Plus a little help from my human, Rusty here. So, what's this half-baked plan of yours to take on Dobie in the dungeon, ay? You'd do better to jump off that cliff out there. Quicker and less painful."

Bouncer approached the corgi. Alice sensed a rift between the pair as wide as the Teviot valley back home.

"I, my little shapeless friend, am Captain. And your captain says we'll storm the dungeon, free Bosona and, once she's been released, her enemies will either flee in terror or join her. General Scratch's orders before he left for the hills. He'll be out there at the back of the palace waiting for the sun to rise before mounting a full-scale attack."

"General Scratch has already lost one army. Seems he's about to lose another."

"Bouncer's right!" interceded the professor.

Alice had almost forgotten about the old man. He had been sitting quietly in a far corner drying his feet, lost in thought. He stood up, holding his shoes, and came between the rival dogs. "And so are you," he added, turning to face George. "It's far too dangerous for Alice to go. I know how you worry about her. And you're wise enough to realise that it's Alice whom we must protect at all costs. I'll go in her place. With you, Bouncer (he swivelled to face the goldador). Bosona knows me. Anyone else, and she might suspect a trap. You're right to fear Dobie, but compared with my mistress in a rage, that goof is like a new-born pup."

"Hmm! Some pup!" scorned George.

Whether the professor was trying to avoid what was fast turning into a dangerous clash between two giant carnivores, or whether there was sense in what he said, the girl could not decide. She only knew that the old man was far from stupid. When he had his shoes back on, the professor, followed by Captain Bouncer and an assortment of dogs, left the kitchen for the stairwell that led down to the depths of the palace and to the dungeon where a monstrous terror, Dobie the Doberman, waited to dismember any living thing that crossed the threshold into his dank, dark domain.

Which left Alice and the remaining humans with George, Carol and Poppy.

Why hadn't Poppy gone with Bouncer? Afraid to spoil her neatly coifed pom-pom? As for George, Alice felt even more uneasy about the corgi after that debacle with her owner. She decided to share her concern with Poppy at the first opportunity.

****

Dylan waited until the wolf was within striking distance of his blade. He held Excalibur above his shoulders (naming his penknife after the most famous sword in history helped to boost his morale) whilst he waved it about in the narrowing space between him and the creature's vast head. A pair of sloping almond eyes, each the size of the cuttlefish bone that he and Caitlin had once found on a beach in Crete, caught flashes of light from the whirling blade.

That bone still had pride of place in his sister's bedroom. As he stood with his back to the wall, he felt ashamed for all the bad things he had ever said to, and about, wee Caitlin. He felt angry with himself, and that anger travelled across his shoulders, down his arms and into the fingers gripped tightly around the handle of Excalibur. The wolf was him, the bad Dylan, the Dylan he never wanted Alice to see. With the strength of the crass Superman imprinted on his rucksack, he slashed with the sword, slicing through the nose of the animal that had him cornered.

Screaming fury, the injured wolf snapped at the boy whose head, lowered by the weight of the sweeping blade, dropped to inches below the huge jaws that bit empty air where, a split second earlier, his face had been. Teeth, the size and colour of bananas, but dagger-sharp, would have made the boy instantly unrecognizable. Instead, Dylan flipped the blade around and thrust it upwards into the neck of the wolf. Blood gushed from a gaping wound as the beast jerked to one side, its massive paw reaching up to ward off further injury. The boy dodged it's fall, only to be confronted by another wolf. His sword seemed heavier when anger was nudged aside by fear. The wolf leapt at him but howled in mid-air and dropped a like a massive brick. A spear was lodged in the back of its hairy neck. Beyond the felled creature stood Ben, feet astride, without his spear. Four wolves encircled him, crouched down, ready to spring, but hesitated. Like Dylan, they must have also felt fear. Finding renewed strength, the boy ran at them, waving Excalibur and screaming:

"Bosona forever!"

Unarmed, Ben did the same. The wolves turned and fled back towards the darkness beyond the poultry hangars.

***

How could she have been so wrong about George? Later, she reckoned it was all about prejudice. Against corgis and dachshunds and other dogs with stumpy legs.

A noise from the stairwell on the landing prompted George and Carol to leave the kitchen. Alice approached the poodle, planning to whisper into a large, beautifully trimmed white ear about her suspicions concerning George. It seemed so obvious to her that the corgi, by going against Bouncer, was the traitor of whom the General spoke. But just as she was about to entrust Poppy with her confidence, the poodle told Rusty, George's pet, to fetch the cambo juice. Alice remained silent, for the poodle's eyes, fringed with delicately curled eyelashes, seemed to bore into her confidence with the precision of dental drills.

Rusty looked at George, his owner, who had just returned to the kitchen, then at Poppy. He barked.

"Go on, be a good boy. Fetch the cambo juice. In that cupboard over there. Hurry!" commanded Poppy.

"Don't!" warned George, but it was too late. His human pet dutifully took down from a shelf a large earthenware jug full of yellow fluid and, with two hands, carried it across the kitchen to Poppy. He snarled as he looked up at her, clutching the jar as if his life depended on it.

"Get Alice to drink the stuff, Rusty. And don't listen to her if she protests." Poppy stood, large and magnificent, between the corgi and his pet. Her black lips parted to reveal two rows of perfectly white, needle-sharp teeth. Her tongue, tinged purple, moved in her mouth before the words emerged: "Pour it down her throat!"

George gaped at the poodle.

"You'll regret this, Rusty," he said. "Be a good human. Tip it out!"

"Ignore Fatso! Just do it," ordered Poppy. Alice, rigid with fear, edged away from the ginger-haired man. When he looked at her, his eyes were as sharp as the teeth of the poodle. "Why should she be allowed to talk whilst you can only bark? Force the cambo juice down her throat if she refuses to drink. Then take her as your slave. Bark at her if she displeases you. Plus, you'll both be able to enjoy the protection of Poppy-the-Great as her two favourite pets. But only if you always do exactly as I say. Understand, my little red-haired human?"

Alice, fearing the lecherous glint in the man's narrowed eyes, had already discovered that these Dogtopian humans, who only barked, did seem to understand the spoken word. She wished and wished and wished that Dylan would suddenly burst out from the sewer with that giant penknife of his. Perhaps Bouncer might have second thoughts, turn around and come bounding back through the door. Neither of these things happened. She pulled the scissors free from her jeans belt and held them up towards Rusty, opening and closing the blades, hoping he'd take fright. The thought of never again being able to talk, only bark, and enslaved to this creature, was somehow worse than that of being savaged by those gleaming poodle teeth.

"Keep back!" she warned.

Someone grabbed her from behind. A hand smashed down on her wrist and the scissors clattered to the floor. Poppy laughed. A cruel, though elegant, laugh.

"Now hold her tight whilst Rusty stops that silly girl's voice forever. Just think, she'll have a nice little bark only for you, Rusty. Got yourself a really cute bitch, now."

Rusty, too, bared his teeth in a grin that seemed to curve from one hair-fringed ear to the other. He came forwards slowly, careful not to spill one drop of the precious juice that would remove the power of speech from this annoying, though delightfully pretty, human girl soon to become his property—inasmuch as one human could be 'owned' by another human in a world of dogs. Someone grabbed Alice's long black hair from behind and tugged at it, forcing her head back. The girl kicked out as Rusty approached.

"Go away!" she shouted.

Poppy laughed again.

"Play with her if you wish, but just silence that voice! Only the Top Dog in this land, so soon to be me, may have a pet with the power of speech. And then only one. That'll be the professor, of course. *My* pet as well, from then on!"

"So, it's you!" accused George. "You all along! The traitor! And to think that Scottie chose you himself."

"Ah, Scottie!" mocked Poppy. "So easy to please. Oh, do get on with it, Rusty. There's a good boy."

Alice watched in horror as the jar of cambo juice was raised up in front of her face. She attempted to clamp her mouth shut, but a strong hand took hold of her lower jaw from behind and held it open in a steely grip. She gurgled and gulped as the cold fluid got tipped into her open mouth.

***

The boys' shared jubilation soon passed. The fleeing wolves halted. Dylan saw why. Dozens of ghostly grey faces with glinting eyes emerged from the darkness beyond the beasts as if summoned by the Devil himself. Ben retrieved his spear from the body of the dead wolf. As the boys stood back to back, the wolves spread out in silence, forming a wide circle of teeth and almond eyes. Slowly, this closed in on them. Dylan became aware of the warmth of their breath.

"I think I love your sister," Dylan whispered.

He knew these were probably the last words he would ever utter, but they had to be said before he got chewed to pieces by a pack of giant wolves. Ben merely grunted. He was too preoccupied with trying to decide which animal to kill first, and how he could use the wolves' immense size to his advantage, as in kung fu, when the timing proved right. If Dylan's arrows had flights, then Ben's scholarly neighbour might have killed a few from a distance. As it was, they only had his spear, which he had retrieved, and Dylan's giant penknife against, possibly, hundreds of Mother Nature's most fearsome weapon: a carnivore's tooth.

To save his strength, Dylan held Excalibur low, trailing the blade over the ground so that its sharp edge flashed in the moonlight. That's when he became aware of a familiar odour: that of Ron the Rott.

So, I was right after all, he thought. *He is the traitor who's gone and betrayed us. I knew Alice was wrong about George. Annoying, yes; traitor, no. Guess she's a lot to learn. Wrong about Colin too. No way is that creep good enough for her. And now I'll never know whether—*

There was a sudden commotion amongst the wolves. A gap appeared in their circle. Where wolf faces, hungry for the blood of two boys from Hawick, had been, there was an empty space. Those faces now lay on the ground, bloodied and lifeless. A brown shadow flitted past, behind the wolves, then darted back again. One wolf leapt at it but missed. Without a sound, the huge shadow brought the wolf down. Then another and another. One well-placed bite from Ron was all that was required. The wolves were in disarray, snarling and snapping as they tried in vain to attack the shadow. Ben looked at Dylan, and his expression informed the other boy that it was now or never. Together they ran at the wolves. Ben used the spear as a lance, thrusting and stabbing at wolf flesh whilst Dylan slashed at limbs, backs and necks with what was once a harmless little souvenir penknife from Edinburgh.

"Thank you, Professor Pringle," he whispered when a fourth wolf fell to his blade.

It was over in minutes. No Wolf Police survived, for those that saw sense, and attempted to flee, were soon brought down by Ron.

Alice was wrong and so was I, Dylan told himself. *Forget his smell. That guy is totally awesome! Best ever!*

"Bouncer and the rest of his unit have already finished off the wolves that crept around the side of the palace," Ron informed them. "Wolves need an open space to attack as a pack, see."

"What about the other humans?" asked Dylan, meaning, of course, Alice and the professor.

"He sent them up the sewer into the kitchen."

"I'm off," the boy said. He turned and ran towards the ledge where he'd left Alice asleep.

"Wait, Dylan!" The younger boy halted. "Just show her respect," shouted Ben. "That's all I ask. She's the best sister you could ever imagine." Perhaps, Dylan wondered, he should have shown Caitlin a little more respect rather than teasing her when she prickled his nerves.

He ran on around the corner where not only the bodies of wolves, but also many BUDS fighters, littered the ledge between the palace wall and the precipice. A few dogs sat panting, some licking their wounds. He saw no humans. One dog stood out. The elegant poodle he had joked about to Alice. She wore her blue cap cocked to one side and bore not a single fleck of blood on her clean white fur.

"Poppy!" he called out, proud to remember her name. She looked round at him; looked for a long time, as if taking in every detail, including his bloodied sword, but said nothing. "Alice? The professor? Have you seen them? Ron says they got sent up the sewer. Is that right?"

"If he says so. But you won't get much from the girl."

"What do you mean?"

"Only barks."

"You're lying."

"Only barks, and now she belongs to me and my new pet human, Rusty, so you might as well forget your little friend. Go home. Go back to Hawick without her."

Rusty? Who the heck—?

If he'd had the strength, Dylan would have run the poodle through with his sword. As it was, in his current state of exhaustion, this would have been suicide. Besides, he had to get to Alice. Even if she now only barked, he would do as Ben told him to. Show her respect. And he would kill who- or whatever Rusty was.

***

Bouncer led the way down the spiral stairs towards the near-total blackness of the palace dungeons. Noses took over. The air grew heavy with the smell of rotting bones, dog shit and urine, mixed with that of meat colonised by flies and unfit for canine consumption. Also, there was something else: the scent of a certain dog, so overpowering that he had to cover his nostrils with a paw. The professor, with his useless little human nose, seemed oblivious to all these aromas. In fact, Bouncer began to wonder why on earth the man had joined them in Dogtopia. Perhaps just to make sure the 'little Earth girl-bitch', as his pet, Alice, was now called in military circles, came to no harm. Indeed, Professor Pringle was a big mystery to not only Bouncer, but seemingly all dogs, both Dogtopian and those of Earthly origin.

Halfway down the staircase, Bouncer stopped. Not because of the smell, or anything he saw or heard. It was something he felt.

Back in Hawick, there was a special bond between Bouncer and his then owner. She always seemed to know when he wanted to go out to play in the garden, and whether he was ready for a walk or needed a bone or toy to chew on. Whenever he felt sad, she would appear, as if from nowhere, to stroke and comfort him. Now, with roles reversed, this 'thing' between them had also reversed. She, his beloved pet, was in danger. He knew it. Yet here he was, bathed in the glory of his very first military victory, about to free the beautiful Bosona. Somehow, the presence of the professor seemed to provide a solution.

"Listen," he whispered to the old man, "I'm worried about my pet. Something might have happened to her. George was acting very strange. He might try to get at me by doing something bad to her. Go back to the kitchen, please. Besides, Dobie's far too dangerous for any human to take on. My victory must have gone to my head."

The professor shrugged his shoulders, turned around and slowly made his way back up the steep stairs, stopping every now and again to catch his breath. When he heard a gurgled scream, he ran for the first time in over one hundred years. On reaching the kitchen doorway, there was no way of telling whether he had arrived in time.

***

Ben knew what he had to do. The idea came to him in a flash

when he and Dylan were surrounded by wolves. He'd noticed a coiled rope on the wall of the duck hangar where bright young Caitlin had left behind a desperate message. At the time he thought little of it. Now, on seeing that deadly circle of canine jaws, he fantasised about swinging like Tarzan, above the wolves, from a rope secured around one of the palace battlements, repeatedly piercing them with his spear. Because of Ron, such a display of acrobatics had become unnecessary, but he had no idea what he might be up against inside the palace. Dogs, unlike cats, were mostly useless at jumping. Unless they were to fly astride giant birds, which seemed highly unlikely, the air would provide him with not only a safe space, but an opportunity for surprise attack.

He returned to the duck hangar. Its occupants remained sound asleep. He found the rope. Thin, but, made from some strange, artificial material, it felt strong. After cutting it free, using the sharp flint he'd kept in his pocket after fashioning the spear, he tested the rope by pulling it between clenched fists, then slung the coils over his shoulder. A row of iron hooks hung from a beam, their purpose in relation to ducks only too clear. Many good Chinese restaurants displayed basted, plucked ducks hanging on hooks, such as these, before ending their dead lives on clients' plates. Anger at the thought of Caitlin hanging, as a basted duck, from one of these, gave Ben the strength he needed. He wrenched two hooks free and slotted them into his belt before taking a final look at his neighbour's feathered message. Spurred on by a determination to rescue her, he headed, in the eerie moonlight, for the palace.

***

Dylan scrambled up the steep slope of the sewer, not caring where he put his feet. He wished he had killed Poppy, for it was now as clear as the water that flowed in the River Teviot in summer months: she was the traitor. Whether, or not, she was in with Bruiser was neither here nor there. He, Dylan Ross, had killed giant wolves, and if any harm had been done to Alice, he would kill the poodle, but for the time being all he could think about was his neighbour's safety.

When he began to slip backwards on the slime running down the sewer, he grabbed at rocks jutting from the wall and ceiling and pulled himself along. He saw a light ahead and, soon, the opening of the kitchen sewer chute into which all waste and rubbish got thrown by the humans. With Excalibur held aloft, and newly found strength, he sprang into a large room crowded with humans. The professor, to his relief, stood in the middle of the kitchen. Before him cowered a red-haired man with a wispy beard. Immediately, Dylan hated him, for Alice, seated on the floor, was looking up at the man with those beautiful eyes displaying an unsettling mix of terror and obedience.

Dylan was about to call out to the girl when Professor Pringle held up his hand. A warning to remain silent. Dylan froze. Inwardly, he pleaded for Alice to say something, to speak, to prove Poppy wrong. He watched as she got up and walked slowly towards the old man. It all seemed so unreal. More like watching a movie. The professor slipped his hand into his pocket and took out a handful of colourful powder which sparkled as if ground from myriads of precious gems. Gently, he tapped Alice's lips. "Nice and wide," he said softly. She obeyed. Her mouth opened wide. He held out his opened hand and blew the rainbow dust between those lips that Dylan so ached to kiss, then told her to breathe in.

Dylan found himself taking in a deep breath as if this might help the professor's magic to work. After that, the boy hardly dared to even blink.

The professor stood stock still for what seemed an eternity, during which time Dylan lived a thousand lives, including one in which he gave private maths coaching to a barking girl.

"Tell me your name, child," the man finally said.

At first Alice seemed too afraid to speak. Rusty, the red-haired man, whimpered and snarled. A strange combination.

"Alice Chang," the girl replied.

Dylan, happier than he'd felt for a very long time, ran from the entrance of the sewer.

"Alice," he shouted.

The girl turned. Again, the professor held up his hand.

"Wait!" he cautioned. "Do not speak to your friend yet, Alice. And only answer my questions if you really can. Otherwise say nothing. Tell me, who is your owner?"

Dylan willed her to say 'Bouncer', and she did.

"Why are you here?"

"Ben. Ben and Caitlin. Duck. Caitlin. Duck. Dylan. Over there. Not Colin. Dylan."

"Good girl. Now give me a sentence."

There was a long period of silence during which Dylan's hand gripped Excalibur so hard his knuckles turned white.

"Dylan's Dad was mean to Bouncer. He... he shouted at my dog. It was horrid."

Wow! thought Dylan. *That's three sentences!*

Dylan wanted to run to her, take hold of her hands and tell her he absolutely agreed with her appraisal of the situation, but he remained rooted to the spot.

"Phew!" the professor exclaimed. "I've never done that before. It really shouldn't have worked, but George said you were in such a state of shock when that cambo juice got forced down your throat that you couldn't even bark. If you had barked, I wouldn't have been able to do a thing."

"She really is cured, then? Won't end up barking?" asked Dylan. The professor nodded.

"There is one problem, though," he said. Alice looked scared. "Not for you, my dear. You're well and truly cured. Because of the crystal I had in my pocket. But I was planning to use it for the other girl. The one you said got turned into a duck. The girl with red hair."

"My sister?" offered Dylan. It seemed one problem had been replaced by another. Professor Pringle looked thoughtful. "But—" He fixed keen eyes on the red-haired human who, visibly trembling, now stared at the floor. "—I have an idea. Alice, do you still have your scissors?"

The girl indicated a group of Dogtopian humans huddled together on the floor. They were passing the scissors between them as if these were a gift sent from heaven, oblivious of the danger Alice had been in because of one of their number. Perhaps, transformed by crystal, the scissors held a secret that these people could sense and were trying to fathom, Dylan thought as he wondered what it was that the professor had in mind.

"Good," said Pringle. "Maybe all hope is not lost then."

"Where's George?" asked the boy.

"Over there in the corner," replied Alice. "I was so wrong about him. He saved my life. He warned me not to bark or try to speak. I knew I couldn't speak, but so wanted to bark at Poppy for what she did. And that ugly human there called Rusty. The one who forced me to drink the stuff." The red-haired man's shifty eyes, half-hidden behind narrowed eyelids, looked away when Dylan scowled at him. The boy found it hard to believe that any sort of a soul, human or otherwise, resided on the other side of those eyes. "Carol's licking George clean. I think—" Alice grinned, then whispered into Dylan's ear: "I think she rather fancies him. Can you imagine?"

"How come George saved your life?"

"When I refused to bark, Poppy said she might as well kill me there and then because 'what use is a guard human who won't bark?'"

"And?"

"George ran at her. Snapped at her ankles. Bit Rusty a couple of times. That's why the stinky little man's shaking like a leaf. Carol joined in too. Poppy's a right coward. She fled back down the sewer. Gone to look for reinforcements, maybe. From BUDS dogs who have swopped sides like her. Or Bruiser's brutes. We can't stay here, Dylan. Just gotta find Caitlin before they do anything awful to her."

Like eat her for Great Dogover?

"Oh, if only Ben were here!" Alice continued.

Guilt slammed into Dylan's brain like a lorry skidding off the A7 and hitting a tree. Guilt for not yet telling the girl about her brother.

"I found Ben. Spoke to him."

Oh dear, he thought on misreading Alice's changed expression. *Oh wow!* He re-thought when she hugged him, held him at arm's length and, with her eyes sparkling a thousand unspoken 'thank yous' (or '*xie-xies*'), began to fire questions:

"Where is he? Is he all right? Why did he go into that room? Is he hurt? What's he look like? Has he eaten? Is he taking care of himself? I mean without me to do things for him?"

"One question at a time, please. But first, he saved my life." Dylan so wanted to add, 'and I saved his too', but reckoned that sounded boastful. He remembered her brother's words, 'respect my sister'. Boasting seemed disrespectful. "And he's sure Caitlin's brooch will lead him to her. He found a message from her."

"In quacks?"

"No. Feathers. Beside the duck lake. CR PAL. Don't you see? 'Caitlin Ross taken to the palace.' He'll find her. But there's no time to lose. We just have to release Bosona then take control of the whole palace."

The professor, who had been listening to every word, humphed.

"Just like that?" he questioned.

The teens from Hawick exchanged looks then fixed gazes on the old man like kids at a magic show waiting for a rabbit to be pulled from a hat. But—no hat... no rabbit.

Chapter 8

With the professor gone, Bouncer smelt the Doberman even more strongly as he and his fellow soldiers approached the dungeons. He had never smelt anything like it, not even in Hawick. A smell heavy with cruelty, worse even than wolf-stink. But there was something else about the dungeon. Something that unnerved him: a different sort of smell, rarely encountered when he was Alice's pet back on Earth. The gut-twisting stench of death.

Great Dog forbid, not that of Bosona, please! the goldador begged. *Nothing bad can happen to the beautiful bitch.* Although he had not yet met her, he knew that, also being a blend of Labrador and golden retriever—and female—she would be supremely beautiful.

He cautioned his soldiers, amongst whom were the irrepressibly optimistic mongrels, Bill and Ben. In Alice's absence, their presence boosted his morale.

Descending step by step, with caution, he periodically stopped to sniff the foul air, unnerved by the silence. At a final twist in the staircase, he saw, in the gloom ahead, iron bars from floor to ceiling, and a gap in these across which lay something dark and very large. He turned and raised a paw, a sign to his co-fighters to remain where they stood.

In a single leap, Bouncer was on top of that mound of dog flesh digging his teeth into the neck of the jailer. But the flesh was cold and no blood oozed into his open jaws. He stood back. Dobie the Doberman had been long dead, his great head almost detached from his vast body where his neck had already been ripped open.

Bosona?

The goldador scrambled over the hillock of dead dog and bounded on into the jail beyond. Most cells were empty, save one, at the end of a long corridor, which contained a dead spaniel with wounds identical to those of Dobie. There was no Bosona, dead or alive.

"Retreat!" he called out. "She's not here. And Dobie's dead."

Bill and Ben came down to check.

"Not here," said Bill.

"Missing," agreed Ben the dog.

"Like he said she'd be," added Bill.

"Because of his pride?" suggested his twin.

"Who and what are you two talking about?" asked Bouncer.

"George. Before we left. Said if we're lucky, Bruiser will get here first."

"Nonsense. Dobie was his jailer."

"Dobie was a dimwit. George said. And Bruiser wanted to impress Bosona, he reckoned. All staged. Gets Dobie to attack Bosona then kills him to win her admiration. Dobie was supposed to be unbeatable, see."

"Tricked her, then. But why did George keep all this from me?" asked Bouncer.

"He didn't. I think your ears were facing the wrong way when he said it, sir. Just before we left the kitchen," Ben informed his superior.

On the stairs they rejoined the other BUDS dogs, much relieved not to have to visit the domain of Dobie the Doberman. All returned to the kitchen. Here, Bouncer was hit with another bombshell. One of his cleverest officers, Poppy the Poodle, had almost succeeded in removing the power of speech from his human pet and had expressed her intention of becoming Top Dog. She was nowhere to be seen, but Alice seemed sure that the traitor might soon return with reinforcements. George, bless him, had saved the day. But for how long?

***

Ben hadn't gone far when the silence was broken by barking. From close behind him. He still had difficulty associating barks with people and speech with dogs. Turning to see an Alsatian, which he took to be Ali, with a human straining at the end of a lead and barking furiously, he halted. Was Ali angry? He thought he had informed his owner about going off to look for his red-haired neighbour. What with the confusion that prevailed following the wolf attack, plus meeting up with Dylan, maybe he had taken too long?

"I met up with—" he began but got no further.

"Get him, boy!" urged the dog, dropping the lead held in his mouth. "You can have his shoes if you kill him."

Not Ali! The voice was wrong. Why had he assumed only rotts and wolves were enemy? The human was long-haired, fit and lean. Freed from the leash, the man started to run. Ben, too, was a fast runner and took off at top speed past the hen hangars, up a ramp that led to the palace gates and what looked like a huge enclosure encircled by a low wall. On reaching this, he halted.

He had hoped to escape the human by leaping over the wall onto trees about thirty feet down as he'd once seen in a Chinese kung fu movie, but what lay stretched out across the centre of the enclosure, with one eye open, encouraged him to back away. The human, still barking, also froze, uncertain not of him but of what he knew to be lying in wait for who- or whatever got thrown over the wall. A cat that made a sabre-toothed tiger look like a cuddly little pet. And that was the only one visible in the hazy moonlight. The Alsatian laughed.

"Take his shoes before feeding him to the cats if you like, only hurry up. I want to get back inside. My belly's crying out for bonahol."

Ben held the spear aloft. The man, thin and wiry, was not an easy target. Even if the spear were to find its mark, the horse-sized Alsatian would easily finish him off. Because of Caitlin, he could not let this happen.

"What's holding you back, boy?" shouted the man's owner. Ben raised his left hand whilst aiming the spear at his lean adversary with his right hand.

"You—me?" he suggested, gesturing. "Friends? No fight?" Alice talking to Bouncer back home in Hawick was one thing. Trying to reason with a barking human in a totally alien dimension, who probably didn't, although perhaps did, understand English, was something else.

A sign of peace? he wondered. The only sign he could think of was that of a cross. Like a priest blessing his congregation, Ben traced a cross in the air with his free hand. The human laughed. Ben did it again. The human creased up with laughter and slapped his thighs. He grinned at Ben. Whatever he did or did not understand, there was a recognition of something in that grin. With a beckoning finger, Ben urged the human to come closer. Still giggling, the man did so. He gave a friendly little bark, as Bouncer used to do when Alice came home from school. Ben held out his hand, palm sideways. Instead of shaking it, the man slapped it and laughed again.

"Useless pet," snarled the Alsatian. "I'll have you put down." In three easy bounds, he reached the two humans, but was unprepared for what happened next. When he pounced, Ben ducked and jabbed the spear upwards at the throat of the dog whilst the man rolled onto the ground and kicked at the belly of the animal. Pivoted on the spear point, the dog shot up and over the wall. There was a bloodcurdling scream, suddenly cut short. Ben, with the spear still in his hand, peered over the wall to see a cat, twice the size of a now headless dog, tearing a twitching canine leg free from its body. He wanted to high-five with the man but decided not to.

If making a cross in the air is some sort of a friendly joke, who knows what raising your hand up, palm forwards, means?

The man looked at Ben, his mouth open, panting and whimpering as if awaiting the next command. Ben had become his new master. For all the boy from Hawick knew, the Alsatian might have been subjecting him to a life of torment and misery, for he was the first human Ben had seen on a leash.

The boy removed the man's collar and leash and flung these into the Pit to join the Alsatian. For good measure, he made another sign of the cross with the same result. The man laughed.

After slipping his hand into his pocket, Ben fingered Caitlin's brooch. His mind immediately pictured a huge hall and a small cage just large enough for a duck. The hall was packed with dogs, mostly asleep, though some stirred. Up against all four walls crouched rottweilers. On a raised platform, where the duck cage stood, the largest of the rotts lay nonchalantly stretched out across a colourful rug. Another dog that looked just like Bouncer, with its legs in chains, lay, by itself, at the other end of the platform.

Urged on by the vision, the Chinese boy ran with his new friend towards the palace. The sky to the east was brightening. Whether or not this was the dawn of Caitlin's last day now depended on him.

***

The professor sat down on the floor with his back to the wall and stared blankly ahead. Dylan showed Alice the feathers and asked if she could use them to make flights for his arrows. He reckoned that, being able pick up tiny bits of food with chopsticks, she would have the required dexterity. The boy marvelled at how those small, graceful fingers, working away, soon filled a quiver (his rucksack) with potentially lethal arrows. Whiskers did not object.

They were sitting together beside the professor. No one spoke. Alice's admiring eyes tried to tell Dylan things his teasing-damaged brain failed to see before he removed Whiskers from his rucksack. He handed the mouse to the girl, then offered the quivering little creature a few crumbs. These were hastily devoured. After he had returned Whiskers to the safety of the rucksack, Alice rested her head on his shoulder. Fearing she might already have done the same thing on Colin's muscle-padded shoulder, he remained stock-still. The girl soon drifted off to sleep, but not Dylan. No chance. He didn't dare move. To disturb her slumber now might have encouraged her to go running off to seek out the dumb rugby forward when back in Hawick.

So, instead of sleeping, he thought about Caitlin. Everyone knew the girl was a brilliant child. Was this why he'd become so antagonistic towards her of late? She sometimes came up with answers to questions way beyond him, despite the fact that he was top of his class. Was it the fact that she no longer looked up to her big brother that annoyed him? Whatever, he sat and brooded, wracked with guilt, his only consolation that his neighbour (*yes*, he decided, *I am definitely in love with her*) was using him as a pillow. Clutching his curved bow to his chest, he wished he could be more like Ben. That boy was awesome. No doubt about it, Ben would rescue Caitlin.

But as a duck?

How could he go home to his parents carrying a red-haired duck and say: "Morning! Oh... by the way, this is Caitlin. You can tell by the hair, see. It's still red!"?

Dylan's mum said her daughter was a true Pict. Living in the Scottish Borders, the boy knew all about the Romans, what with the Trimontium Museum in Melrose, but Picts, and Celts as the Romans called the locals, were a mystery to him. Apart from some of them painting their faces. Caitlin had not been impressed when he suggested to her that she should go around with a Saltire on her face, as in Braveheart, on the day of the Scottish Independence Referendum.

She'd become very self-critical about her appearance of late, particularly if she thought she might be seen by their Chinese neighbour. The boy, not the girl. In a shop in the High Street, she had once spent nearly an hour deciding on which lipstick colour best complemented her hair. Two years back, she would have asked Dylan for advice. Not now.

Thinking about these things, all Dylan wanted was to have his little sister back, annoying and picking on him. Especially picking on him. Otherwise, like that duck, it wouldn't truly be Caitlin.

Professor Pringle suddenly leapt to his feet as if snapping out of a deep dream. "No time to lose," he announced. Dylan shook Alice awake.

"Where—oh!" she exclaimed as if disappointed to see that Dylan, not Colin, had been her support.

"You've been asleep," said Dylan. "And thanks for—you know—for these." He ran his hand over the stems of the arrows protruding from the rucksack.

"Promise me you'll take care of Whiskers," she said.

She really does care about animals. Maybe that's why she likes Colin.

Dylan, now standing, offered Alice a hand, but she got up on her own. His tree shrank.

"He'll be quite safe," he said.

"You did say he's got a spear?"

"Whiskers?"

"No! I was thinking about Ben. Or dreaming. Not sure."

"You were definitely asleep."

"Do you think much about your sister?"

There must be a right answer, reckoned Dylan.

"Yes. All the time. Ben *will* rescue her. I know it."

"But what if something happens to my brother. I couldn't bear it."

"He'll be fine."

"Don't you humans ever stop talking?" It was George. His wounds, licked clean by Carol, were already healing. The other dogs were ready to go, each with a dutiful human at his or her side. Even children seemed to belong to the dogs. Two were playing tag around a patient pooch's legs.

"The general will have arrived. Now is the only time." The professor was looking at Dylan as he said this.

"Only time for what?"

"To climb the Tower."

"Tower?" Dylan had no idea what Professor Pringle was talking about. "Is my sister in a Tower."

"No. Nor, I hope, anyone or anything else. Not in the lead-up to Great Dogover. That's why it's our only chance. He might have got there first, though. To gloat."

"Who?"

The professor studied the boy for a few moments, as if trying to decide how it could be that the boy was so stupid.

"Scissorman, of course!"

***

The man was far from stupid. His eyes glinted like jewels whilst Ben explained, in a mix of simple speech and sign language, how they should scale the wall of the palace using his rope and tackle, enter through an upper floor window and, with most palace dogs lying sozzled in the Great Hall, make their way to a balcony. 'Balcony' was a stumbling block. The more he tried to explain with his hands, the more puzzled the man appeared. Which is when he decided to name the guy 'Tarzan'.

"Me Ben, you Tarzan," he said, with the appropriate hand gestures. A rather skinny Tarzan woofed. A sure sign, Ben reckoned, that he appreciated his new name.

The palace was high. Higher than any building he'd seen in the Scottish Borders. Indeed, there was nothing to equal its size either in China or Edinburgh. Even her lofty castle, perched on an extinct volcano, would have fitted many times into the Grand Palace of Dogtopia. Tall towers punched at the sky like fists of stone, with one, sporting a crenelated masonry crown, higher than the rest.

Caitlin's brooch informed Ben that the girl was in the centre of the building and terrified out of her wits. He fixed the hooks to the rope then, like a Hollywood cowboy, whirled this in widening circles before launching it at a window a third of the way up. It flew, trailing the rope, between bars in the window, spun and hooked itself fast around one of these. Ben tugged to make sure it held firm, then, pulling himself up, stepped upwards against the grey wall and slowly made his way towards the window. Once there, he pointed to the rope.

"Tarzan's turn now," he called down. Ben's accomplice proved to be quite a gymnast, almost running up the side of building. From the window, they reached a balcony, higher up—a balcony with an open door leading into the palace.

They found themselves in a large bedroom without beds. Instead, there were three dog baskets, two huge, and one smaller (paddling pool-sized). It seemed they had entered the sleeping quarters of an eminent Dogtopian family. Because of the festivities, like other palace residents these dogs would now be in the Great Hall, sloshed senseless with bonahol, and looking forward to the annual two-day madness which was due to commence after first light.

The corridors were wide. Wide enough to accommodate sleeping Dogtopian guards. Not even an explosion, or the pong of Ron the Rott, would have roused them from their alcoholic stupor, but Ben was taking no chances. Silent as shadows, he and Tarzan crept past the prostrate, canine bodies. No sonic detector would have been sensitive enough to pick up the soft tread of their feet on the cold stone floor.

Halfway along the corridor was a door that opened onto a wide spiral staircase. This wound upwards with so many turns that Ben was beginning to feel dizzy when, at last, they emerged onto a wide balcony that ran the length of the high wall of the Great Hall. As Caitlin's red brooch had informed Ben, the huge space below was packed with drunken, dozing dogs. The boy no longer needed the brooch to locate Caitlin. She had been squashed into a small cage, on a platform, in front of the dark brown hulk of usurper Top Dog Bruiser. Nearby, shackled and stretched out, lay a majestic goldador almost identical to Bouncer. Even from a distance, Ben could see that the duck cage was securely fixed, with a large padlock, to a chain. Behind Bruiser squatted two subservient humans with their heads sunk forwards. As for poor wee Caitlin, she was so confined that her red-haired duck's head was pressed up against the top of the cage. She barely had space enough to breathe in and out.

Ben had to cool a rush of anger that threatened to expose him and ruin Caitlin's chances of rescue. So far, he had not been spotted, and certainly not by Caitlin, although from her fidgety movements and wide-open, frightened eyes, he could tell she was awake. The only chance of a rescue would be for him to swoop down, during the turmoil of battle, after Ali, Bouncer and General Scratch had launched their three-pronged attack.

Luckily, the high balcony was otherwise empty. Without knowing, Ben and Tarzan had chosen a hiding place out of bounds to all dogs during the Feast of Great Dogover. A longstanding tradition dictated that during the two-day run-up to Great Dogover, and on the day itself, no living creature should be at a level higher than that of the Top Dog. Normally, the long balcony was alive with activity, day and night. Bosona had, during her term of office, ignored what she regarded as piffling elitism, but the present brutal leader threatened the Pit to all who disobeyed.

Ben had hoped to grab a little more sleep on the balcony, but on seeing Caitlin, so alone, so vulnerable, he barely blinked for fear of missing any opportunity to save her life.

***

The professor knew that no palace dog nor human would dare be on a level above the floor of the Great Hall. Rusty was essential to his plan which, he had to admit, had little chance of success. However, being a scientist, he liked to experiment. Even if he'd had an ample supply of crystal, experimenting was all he could do. But Professor Pringle did admire Dylan's cool-headedness. Plus, he could tell how fond the boy really was of his little sister who had been cruelly turned by Scissorman into a special duck. Such love might, he believed, amplify the power of any crystal he could lay his hands on. And he prayed to the Great Dog that the experiment would work.

Rusty, with his wrists bound, was slung over George's broad back like a sack of vegetables. A column of dogs and humans who could be trusted (here, Alice's feminine instinct proved invaluable) ascended the stairs to the next level. They split into two groups. Alice and the professor, accompanied by the corgis and their loathsome red-haired burden, continued on up the stairs to the Tower—up and up and up. Meanwhile, Dylan, Bouncer and the rest of his special unit filed out into the corridor that ran alongside the Great Hall. Dylan wanted to launch an offensive as soon as he spotted the tiny duck cage on the platform, but Bouncer, as if reading his mind, shook his head. Instead, they found spaces where they could lie down in between snoring palace dogs and their human pets and feign sleep. Each kept one eye open, prepared to spring into action.

***

151

The burst of yells and shouts were at first assumed to be Great Dogover revellers suffering the effects of bonahol.

"Can't they just sleep? I'm really shattered," Dylan overheard one of the rott guards say. Then he smelt an all too familiar smell and gave Bouncer a nudge with his elbow, a wink and a thumbs-up.

"What a stink!" exclaimed the guard's companion.

"It's okay. That's genuine rott. Only a bit strong. That's all."

"All? It's enough to wipe out every flipping rebel in Dogtopia!"

And the guard laughed his last laugh, for behind him a burst of screams and human barking could in no way be attributed to an extension of the drunken orgy of the night before. Through bonahol-bleared eyes, he saw not only fit, fighting dogs leaping over prostrate fellow rotts and wolves, biting at necks and limbs, but also strange dogs who rose up from their midst and sank teeth into peaceful palace dog flesh. Both guards soon lay dead. Some rotts fought bravely and began to drive back the invaders, only to be met by a fresh attack from the other end of the hall. Bruiser leapt from the platform and immediately proved his worth as a fighter. Many rebel dogs turned and fled from his fearsome teeth. That is, until a new threat to his authority appeared, backed by a sizeable army of dogs wearing blue BUDS caps, and led by a giant of a dog with a basin on his head.

Dylan marvelled to see the enormous bulk of General Scratch carve a path through the rotts and wolves who had gathered protectively around their Top Dog. One by one, they were tossed aside by the St Bernard's massive jaws until he came face to face with Bruiser in the centre of the Great Hall. Meanwhile, the boy proved Alice's worth as an arrow maker with his bow. Propelled by the taut underpants' elastic, her arrows shot straight and true. When he aimed at a head, an arrow soon pierced that same head. Not as devastating as the damage wreaked by the teeth of the larger dogs, but enough to considerably weaken the foe.

Whilst the two titans, Bruiser and General Scratch, circled each other within a widening ring of dogs eager to see which way this very personal fight would go before joining the fray, Dylan, with only one arrow left in his Superman quiver, saw, to his horror, that the cage on the platform was empty. Flapping and struggling to break free, a funny-looking duck with a tuft of red hair, was being held upside down by a human female. He'd seen this woman before in the company of that weasel, Rusty. His wife, perhaps? Bosona remained still and useless, with chains tight around her legs, but it was another dog up there on whom the boy now fixed his archer's gaze. A prim white poodle.

Poppy fluttered her long black eyelashes, strutting across the platform as if the 'to-the-death' battle between Bruiser and Scratch was of little importance. Suddenly she stopped. She approached Caitlin. The little duck stopped flapping as the dog sniffed her all over. Poppy turned to face the crowd, more and more of whom had ceased fighting. Even those who had been keenly watching the present Top Dog taunt the General now faced the platform and seemed eager to hear the elegant poodle speak. A hush swept through the hall, broken only by the grunts of the two great fighters as they snapped and swiped at each other.

"Neither of those two can win," she shouted in a thin, clear voice as sharp as a razor. "They are both, what you might call, spent forces. And as for Bosona here, well you can all see for yourselves what sort of a leader she's become. Ha!" she exclaimed scornfully. "She couldn't even lead a pack of human puppies. We'll not waste any of this very special treat on her, shall we? Not when there's barely a mouthful to be had. As for keeping her alive in the Bitch Ditch as Bruiser had planned—it's a waste of precious space. She and all those other bitches who fail to bow down to me will get thrown to the cats in the Pit."

A stupid dog cheered. Then another and another. Dylan's rage with the poodle who so nearly lost Alice her power of speech hit the gong. Unseen by any dog, he raised his bow, drew his last arrow back till the flint tip rested on the thumb of his bow hand, aimed for Poppy's cruel-though beautiful-eye and let it fly.

With the eye being soft, the arrow sank in deep. Poppy screamed and raised a paw to her stricken face. Angered dogs focused on Dylan who dropped the bow and started to stab and slash with Excalibur. A wave of gasps swept through the hall. Something happened up on the platform. Poppy had fallen to her side, with a spear lodged in her chest. It must have pierced her heart, or what she had of one, for within moments she stopped moving. A few breaths later, and her chest went still. The woman holding the 'special' duck looked confused until, uttering a loud jungle cry, Ben swung down from the balcony and, in one continuous movement, seized the duck and knocked the woman to the ground. The man called Tarzan quickly followed and, yelping like a happy puppy, freed Bosona from her chains.

In the chaos that reigned, Dylan pushed through a crowd of confused dogs and shouted to Ben. Ben yelled back, and both boys left the Great Hall in the paws, so to speak, of the rightful Top Dog, whilst they scaled the stairs two at a time to seek out Alice and the professor. Never, before, had Dylan-the-nerd run like this, but he was running to save his sister from spending the rest of her otherwise short life as a duck in a land of duck-eating dogs.

***

The steps to the Tower went on and on, up and up, but neither Ben nor Dylan slowed until they heard voices ahead. Dylan recognized the carefully chosen speech of George and the stuttered words of the professor. He was thankful to hear Alice who said:

"Hand over the key, Scissorman, or my brother will make you regret it."

Hugging the duck, Ben stayed put, for no way was he going to allow Scissorman to touch Caitlin again. Dylan rounded the last bend alone to see the black-cloaked figure glide to-and-fro in front of a heavy, dark oak door. The spectre had a large key in his long, spindly fingers. The key to the Tower. The professor held out his hand, urging the creature to give him the key. The figure's hood was hollow and black. The red eyes, of which others had spoken, weren't there. The boy remembered being told how Scissorman's face came and went depending on his strength. The loathsome fiend also badly needed crystal. Whilst the battle was going on in the Great Hall, he had sneaked up the stairs and overcome the key bearer, a human, only to be confronted by his arch enemy, Professor Pringle.

Weakened, Scissorman wasn't going to waste energy by speaking. Besides, he didn't seem to have a mouth. George ran at him and tried to bite his legs, but the corgi's teeth

155

merely closed around empty space. Carol did the same, but it proved to be their undoing for the bites seemed to enfeeble the dogs and strengthen Scissorman. The red eyes began to glow again, the fingers got longer. The dogs lay on the ground, unable to stand, whimpering and muttering as Scissorman reached out with his free hand and curled long spindly fingers around the professor's scrawny neck. The old man choked and gurgled and flailed his arms. Dylan attempted to stab the flowing black cloak with the point of Excalibur. If ever he needed a magical sword, now was the moment, for there appeared to be nothing inside the cloak.

Alice stepped forward with her mother's scissors wide open. The boy shouted:

"No Alice, he's too dangerous."

Being a girl, she didn't listen.

"Girls, ay!" Ben exclaimed later when told what happened. Calmly, his sister snipped at the fingers clutching the key. It clattered to the ground. Two snips later, and the same scissors had also cut through Scissorman's fingers encircling the professor's neck. Professor Pringle stepped away from the spectre, taking in deep breaths, rubbing at where those steely digits had come so close to strangling him. Scissorman stopped moving. The red eyes went dim, then extinguished. The cloak shrank. It became smooth and shiny, like the back of a beetle. When reduced to the size of a cockroach, the figure dropped onto all fours and scuttled away, past Ben and a duck of Scissorman's making, before disappearing under the door.

Alice stood with her mouth agape, unable to believe what she had just done. The key lay on the stone floor. Those spaghetti fingers, like their owner, had vanished. Grinning insanely, Dylan picked it up.

"That was so cool, Alice. Man, you were brave!" At this point, Ben joined them...

"Did she just, um—?" he began to ask Dylan. The younger boy nodded.

"Girls, ay!" was all Ben could say.

"Oh, stop messing around, you two. Help the professor!" scolded Alice. "The key, Dylan. Use it!"

Feeling like reprimanded child, Dylan snapped the key into the lock and gave it a twist. The door groaned open, as if reluctant to reveal its guarded secret. Beyond, a ladder was propped up against a wooden ledge.

***

Bouncer joined the ring of dogs encircling the two great fighters: Scratch, the champion through sheer size, and Bruiser, the fearless muscle-packed master of brutality. No other dog dared to get close to the pair, though Bouncer longed to have a go at the rottweiler after seeing how poorly Bosona had been treated. He waited and watched, his tongue hanging out as often it used to back in Hawick.

Bruiser, impatient, attacked first. He darted forwards, but before his cruel jaws could clamp their teeth into one of the St Bernard's tree-like legs, a paw the size of a boulder slammed him aside, making the rott squeal like a pig. Bouncer and his blue-capped soldiers laughed and the palace dogs, worried, looked at each other. Bruiser stood up again then walked around the larger dog, trying to decide on Plan B. The general remained static, apart from the occasional slight turn of his majestic head as he followed his rival with his eyes.

Something unexpected happened. Something that extracted gasps of horror from some dogs and shrieks of delight from others. Bruiser, in one easy bound, leapt onto the General's magnificent back. With all four legs splayed out, the smaller animal maintained his grip before sinking his teeth into the larger one's neck.

For a few moments, Bouncer held his breath, his mouth still open. Saliva drooled onto the marbled stone. And not only the goldador's. The floor of the Great Hall was slowly turning into a skating rink of canine spittle as Bruiser attempted to close his mouth around folds of thick, fur-covered canine flesh. At first the general only swayed a little. No one could have guessed the teeth of a giant rottweiler were making their way towards vital structures deep inside that flesh.

Suddenly a chorus of gasps of both horror and delight resonated in the Hall, but the opposite way around. The previously delighted howled from shock whilst the despairing now cheered the huge St Bernard who, without warning, simply rolled onto his back. Calmly, he remained like this with his paws sticking up whilst the rott's struck out at empty space from underneath several tons of dog. The usurper's limb jerks and twitches slowed, then ceased. General Scratch heaved himself off the squashed Rottweiler and onto his side. Bruiser did not move. There was no life left in those evil eyes.

But Scratch had also gone quiet. When Bouncer ran to him, he skidded. The smell on the floor was not that of saliva. The goldador looked down and saw that he'd slipped on a slick of blood oozing from the General's neck.

"Sir, are you all right?" he stupidly asked, for it was clear to all that the general was dying. It required an enormous effort for the St Bernard's large eye to open and focus on the questioner. An even greater effort for the vast mouth to form words:

"Bouncer... good soldier. Makings of a—" Scratch attempted to raise his head but had to give up. "A general," he added. "General Bouncer." His eyelid closed. His chest went still.

Immediately, all remaining BUDS dogs turned on the foe. Humans, armed with spears, also used them with effect, and soon the Great Hall battleground was littered with canine corpses. In a fit of rage, Bouncer tore into what remained of the enemy force until he felt a gentle tug on his tail. He smelt George and turned to face the corgi, also bloodied. The plump dog, eager to join the fight, had left the others in the Tower.

"The rest of us can finish them off, Bouncer," suggested George.

"General Bouncer!" corrected the goldador. "Scratch's dying words,"

But George was looking beyond Bouncer.

"Not if you allow *him* to take over."

George's nose pointed at the stage where Ali was standing above Bosona. The goldador bitch, cowed by weeks of captivity and enchainment, crouched below the Alsatian. Her tail was not wagging. Whatever was happening, or about to happen, up there, was without her consent. Bouncer saw red, leapt over the dead and dying, and bounded onto the platform. Ali's nose picked up on his scent. The Dogtopian dog turned and eyed the Earth dog with scorn.

"Can't you see you're disturbing me and my bitch?" he snarled. "You can go back home now. Become that little girl's pet again. Follow her around on a lead. Safer for a pup like you."

Bouncer bared his fangs. That he loved Bosona was without question. He would die protecting her if he had to.

Ali, on realising yet another tedious skirmish was necessary, left Bosona and faced the goldador with a blood-smeared smirk hanging on his jaws. An experienced fighter, and the larger of the two animals, he knew he could make quick work of this one before subduing Bosona and taking over as Top Dog. In fact, it was going to be so easy, he decided to enjoy himself and play with Bouncer.

"Are you any good at dancing?" he asked. Bouncer said nothing. He crouched low. Ali took this as a mark of subservience. "Oh yes, I'll make you bow to me before I finish you off, Earth dog, but first can you dance like this?"

Ali raised himself up onto his hind legs, flopped his front paws in front of his proud chest and primly pirouetted around like a human ballerina. Some of the BUDS dogs, done with the battle, cheered him on. Others began to taunt Bouncer. But the goldador remained static, tense as a coiled spring. He glanced at Bosona whose nose and eyes were anxiously fixed on him. Ali dropped down and rolled onto his back, kicking his legs in the air.

"Or like this?" he teased.

Still Bouncer did not move.

"How about—?" The Alsatian alternately wiped each side of his face with a paw. "How about wiping away the tears and running off with your tail between your legs like a good little puppy and leaving me and Bosona to get on with the Mummy and Daddy dog stuff?"

Bouncer merely stared at his larger rival when Ali spun around like a clown, chasing his own tail.

Puppy? thought Bouncer. *Yes, carry on playing the puppy, chum!*

The goldador remembered feeling dizzy and disorientated doing the same thing as a puppy, with Alice, in the park. She had a friend with her, and she and the friend were doing cartwheels and handstands and spinning around. After Bouncer had tried to copy her, he staggered about for a few moments.

The Earth dog sprang at the Alsatian, knocking him off balance. In a flash, the rebel leader's neck was opened. Blood spurted. The surprise in Ali's eyes was quickly replaced by the sightless gaze of death. Dogs who had made fun of Bouncer fell silent. The goldador bounded over to join Bosona. For several minutes, with both dogs wagging their tails, they sniffed, then licked each other.

"Who *are* you?" the bitch finally asked.

"Bouncer. Now General Bouncer, Your Dogship. At your service!" Bosona stood up, shaky at first. She was a little smaller than Bouncer, but their colour and markings were identical.

"Thank you, Bouncer, but you're more than a general to me. Without you being here to save me, I'd have probably given myself to the cats in the Pit rather than to that Alsatian."

George eased his bulk up onto the platform and waddled over to the goldadors.

"Your Dogship," he said to Bosona, "for a while we've all felt you have need of a companion to protect you from another Bruiser situation. Surely a general like Bouncer would fit the bill?" Neither Bouncer nor Bosona needed his persuasion. They proceeded to lick each other all over before Bouncer, awash with confidence, turned around to stand beside their freed leader and face the crowd. Bosona spoke first:

"Brave rebels, BUDS comrades and loyal palace dogs who helped defeat the evil usurper, Bruiser, thank you everyone. I pronounce General Bouncer my new second-in-command and—" The goldador bitch paused and looked sideways at Bouncer. "—And my new-found partner." A cheer swept through the audience. "We will rule together with fairness and justice for all dogs."

George looked as if he had something more to say.

"What is it, George?" asked Bosona.

"Your Dogship," the corgi began, "what about the Pit?"

"Ah, the cats, ay?" Bosona glanced sideways at Bouncer. "Before Bruiser appeared on the scene, the professor was experimenting with crystal. Seeing whether he could change its configuration in a way that would shrink the cats. Make them smaller even than humans."

"Wow!" exclaimed a droopy-eared dachshund called, unsurprisingly, Droopy. "That sounds so cool!"

"May I speak?" asked Bouncer.

"My general wishes to speak," the beautiful bitch announced.

"Fellow Earth dogs, you have a choice", shouted Bouncer. "Either you remain here with us and help rebuild the glory that was once Dogtopia, or you return to Earth with the two Earth boys. It's up to you. The professor and the girl, my pet, will of course be staying."

George appeared uneasy. "The girl?" he queried.

"Yes. As I said, she's my pet. She stays here. Because the professor has another plan. Involving your pets. You've all seen how helpful it's been to have these talking humans with us. So, Professor Pringle, after sorting out the cats, will try to give speech to other Dogtopian humans. To do this, he'll need Alice here. For the experiments."

"Talking humans?" yelled a terrier standing next to Droopy. "Is that sensible?"

"Indeed, it is," answered Bosona. "I couldn't do without *my* talking pet, the professor, and Bouncer will keep his talking human. Why shouldn't you lot also benefit from talking pets?"

"But Your Dogship... I mean—" began George, not knowing quite how to put his question. "I mean, is this what *she* wants? Alice?"

Annoyance distorted Bouncer's features.

"Great Dog, she's my pet! Why should I be taking orders from a pet?"

"Hear, hear!" murmured a group of dogs near the platform.

"But—" George's confusion was apparent. "But she's not from this dimension. Not used to being a pet. Surely—"

"Do not disobey!" roared Bouncer. "My pet stays with us. The professor will need her for his experiments! A sacrifice I'm prepared to make for all our futures. Fetch her at once. Where are those humans, anyway? And the professor? What's he up to? Have the Earth humans stolen him?"

George glanced at Bosona who looked Bouncer for a reply.

"What if Alice doesn't want—?" he began.

"Fetch her!" snapped Bouncer. "The boys can leave. Together with any EDD dogs who'd prefer to be slaves to humans rather than the other way around. All those who stay may choose pets from barking humans whose owners died in battle. And with luck, and a little help from my pet, the professor may soon have them talking for all of you."

None wanted to leave.

A plan formed inside George's head. Once outside, he headed for the Greys' Lounge, the next floor down, rather than going to the Tower, as instructed, to fetch Bouncer's pet.

Chapter 9

Dylan knew what he had to do. He removed his rucksack (*at least she hasn't yet teased me about that bloody Superman*) and took out his keychain to which was attached a small torch. He checked that this still worked then glanced at Alice, hoping, perhaps, to see a flicker of admiration, but all he saw was determination to save his own sister from an unimaginably awful fate.

Ashamed to be wishing for anything more, he carefully placed Caitlin's red dress and undergarments on the floor then took the mouse, wrapped in his hankie, out of his rucksack pocket for Alice to look after. With the empty rucksack slung over one shoulder, he climbed the first three ladders. The others, Alice included, stood staring up at him. Before he disappeared into the darkness of the Tower to find more raw crystal for the professor, he heard the girl call out: "Please take care."

She cares about me? Or is she only concerned about the crystal? Dylan's brain couldn't decide which.

Normally the Tower was heavily guarded twenty-four hours a day. Scissorman had known it would be unguarded in the run-up to Great Dogover and would have been hoping to make off with as much of the magical material as would fit into the deep pockets of his black cloak. Instead, Dylan would now fill his rucksack with whatever was needed to give Caitlin back her human life. "As much as you can carry," the professor had said.

After scaling the first three ladders, it became so dim that the boy had to use his key-ring torch. Each time he thought he was at the top, another ladder connecting to a further level appeared in the gloom. He reckoned the ladders were all about thirty feet long. After he had counted ten, it started to get brighter. He trod softly, in case a large dog, or something even more malevolent, stood guarding the crystal.

The topmost level could only be reached by squeezing through a square hole out of which flowed a soft yellow light. Dylan only just managed this, fully aware that should the ladder fall, or get removed by hidden hands, he could die alone up there.

The boy no longer had need of the torch. For a few magical moments, he stood in the high-ceilinged loft of the Tower staring at a great wooden chest on the floor. Its lid was open. Inside were a dozen or so gleaming, golden nuggets. At least, that's what they appeared to be until he realised the colour was wrong. It was more lemon than gold, and, as he approached, and looked from different angles, there were subtle changes in hue. Sometimes he saw a hint of blue, then, as he walked in a circle around the chest, he also saw green, mauve and orange. Furthermore, even when he stood still, the nuggets continually altered shape as if pulsing with a mystical, universal rhythm. Nothing he had learned in science at Hawick High School prepared him for this. Would this strange material provide the key for his sister's release from torment as a duck?

There was also an odd smell and although he saw no one else—no dogs or other creatures—he had a feeling that something or someone was watching. Hurriedly, he stuffed the nuggets into his rucksack, turned around and there he was:

Scissorman... tall, his eyes on fire, his fingers re-grown.

"Boy, hand me that bag with the crystal you've stolen, and I may let you live. I shouldn't, of course, for taking that silly little red-haired duck away from the dogs, but—well, I've a kind heart, right?"

"Out of my way," warned Dylan. "I'll never forgive you for what you did to my sister."

"Oh, is that who the little duck is? Or was! Glad to be rid of her, I'll bet."

"No! I love her. She's family."

The closeness between Alice and her brother entered his brain. He felt even more ashamed of all the bad things he'd ever said to, or about, his sister. He really did love Caitlin.

"Pssst!" hissed Scissorman.

The cloak and the eyes started to glide towards him. Thankfully the ladder was still there.

Not so clever, are you, Mr Scissorman? Dylan thought. *Had you pushed away that ladder, I'd be totally in your power.*

Dylan edged sideways towards the hole in the floor and the ladder. Scissorman stretched out his arms, reaching with noodle fingers that cut through the air, feeling, testing—seeking out an impertinent boy from the Scottish Borders who dared to challenge his authority.

When those fingers seemed to have difficulty in locating him, something occurred to Dylan. Scissorman was blind. His senses were concentrated in the long fingers wavering like the antennae of a giant insect. The red eyes were merely decoration. After having his fingers snipped off by Alice's scissors, the monster had been disabled but, like the tails of certain lizards the boy had read about, they had re-grown. Their source of power had to be crystal, all of which was now in his rucksack. He slipped this off his shoulder and held it up with one hand. It was heavy, but he needed his other hand free. This he rested on Excalibur.

"Don't you recognize the picture on my bag?" he asked.

Scissorman only hissed as faltering fingers sought out the owner of the voice.

"Oh, you poor thing!" the boy exclaimed. "You're blind! I am so sorry."

"Last chance," warned Scissorman. "Hand over what's mine... mine... mine!"

The voice faded with each repeated word into a hiss of foul breath. Silently, the boy from Hawick pulled Excalibur from his belt and held it high. How he had the strength to hold this, plus the ton-weight rucksack, in separate hands, he had no idea. He only wished he could have recorded himself on his Smart phone, still plugged in beside his bed back in Hawick, for Alice's sake.

"The picture on my bag. Superman," Dylan told Scissorman. "Heard of him?" Another hiss. The fingers were only a foot or so away, slicing through air so thick with the creature's breath that, if the boy had had a free hand, he could have grabbed a fistful of the stench. "*I'm* Superman!" he cried out before springing backwards.

The fingers slashed out at where Dylan had been when he spoke. Excalibur sliced down like Madame Guillotine. Dylan had enjoyed reading about that period in French history, never thinking that a Guillotine could be put to good rather than evil use. A blood-curdling shriek ricocheted off the confined walls of the Tower loft. Way below, Dylan heard a girl's anguished voice cry out...

"Dylan?"

It sounded so very far away, but...

At least she cares!

The boy did not wait for the fingers on Scissorman's other hand to regain control. He ran at the hand. A second later, five more finger-noodles squirmed on the floor like helpless worms, shrinking all the time. The cloak also shrank, as when Alice, with her earlier demonstration, had shown him what to do. The red lights that Dylan had taken for eyes vanished, and the hood became a fading blank space.

"Nah! Don't think you'll need any more crystal, Mr Scissorman. See ya!" But Dylan could only hope and pray that he'd truly seen the last of the evil spirit with scissor fingers as he scrambled down the ladders, one by one, with the loaded rucksack on his back and the giant penknife back in his belt.

Alice's relief and admiration were obvious to all but Dylan when he jumped from the bottom ladder to join them.

"What was that awful sound?" she asked.

"Oh, just Scissorman getting what he asked for. And not getting what he wanted!"

"I thought he got turned into a beetle. That little black thing that ran away."

Dylan lowered the rucksack to the ground then opened it out for all to see the glistening crystal nuggets.

"Some beetle! Must've got turned back with some of this stuff," he replied.

"Wow!" exclaimed Alice. "So, you were up there all alone, like... with... with *him?*"

Dylan grinned shyly, for the 'all alone' resounded with feminine approval. His confidence tree almost touched heaven.

"It was nothing! But thanks for showing me how to disable him," he added. "If you hadn't cut his fingers off, I'd never have thought of that. The professor might've had two ducks on his hands. Or rather, a duck and a drake."

"Dylan, bring Rusty over here," said the professor. "Quick!"

The red-haired Dogtopian human lay cowering up against the wall. Although Dylan wanted to punch the wiry little man for what he did to Alice, it was because of Alice that he didn't. Not wishing to appear vindictive, he untied the Dogtopian's bonds and helped him up. Rusty whimpered with fear.

"Now's your chance to make amends to my friend, Alice," Dylan told him. If he'd read the esteem written across the girl's face, his confidence tree would have filled the Universe. "Please help my sister," he requested.

"Alice, I need your scissors," said Professor Pringle. Alice handed him the scissors. "And you, Dylan, use the flat of your penknife blade to crush the crystal into a powder. Every fragment. Until it glows like gold."

"Let me help," suggested Alice. Dylan felt shattered, but he did not want her to think Colin would have found it a doddle.

"I'll be fine," he replied. "Just talk to Caitlin. Tell her she's gonna be okay."

Whilst Dylan used every ounce of remaining energy in his exhausted, nerd-muscles to reduce the crystal nuggets to powdered golden dust, Alice, still stroking Whiskers, talked to Caitlin. She told the younger girl-come-duck that they would change her back very soon, that she would be fine and that they would all return to Hawick as if nothing had happened. Perhaps it was just as well that she was still unaware of her pet-turned-owner's intention of keeping her forever imprisoned in Dogtopia as part of a grand experiment to enable all Dogtopian humans to talk.

***

George knew that there was no time to lose. He flopped down the stairs as fast as his stumpy legs would allow, bumbled along the corridor and into the Greys' Lounge.

The corgi had no idea what sort of a reception he might get, for the greyhounds were a law unto themselves. The fact that they were lounging about, telling each other jokes and boasting of their prowess at the races, was testimony to this. Whilst every other palace pooch had taken part in the festivities and the battle, for greyhounds Great Dogover was a total non-event. Why should they be interested when it didn't involve speed? Had palace top knobs not taken such an interest in betting at the races, they would've all been heaved over the wall into the Pit for insubordination. As it was, they were the one species of dog that enjoyed privileges, whatever they did or said.

One of them deigned to look at George when he entered but did not raise his head from the ground. "What's Fatso doing in our Lounge?" he asked.

"I have a challenge for you," replied George.

The greyhound chuckled.

"Me against a podgy corgi?" he queried. "I love it! Griselda, have you ever heard anything so funny?"

Griselda, more serious than the others, got up and walked on her long runner's legs over to the corgi. She sniffed the top of his head, his broad back and his tail.

"He's all right," she remarked. "What sort of a challenge?" she asked.

"Speed," George replied simply. Several greyhounds laughed, though not Griselda.

"Speed's what we're about, dude!" remarked one. "But it's no challenge to us."

"It is when the bloodhounds are after you."

Before the wolves had been brought in, the bloodhounds acted as Dogtopian special police. Although they couldn't match greyhounds for speed, they possessed stamina second to none. Their incredible noses ensured that they never lost the scent of their prey, and they simply kept on running until the quarry had been brought to heel. Or rather, to justice. Success was measured not by whether the culprit was caught, which invariably he or she was, but how quickly this came about. The challenge for the greyhounds would be not only to outrun the bloodhounds but to outwit them.

The laughter stopped. Another greyhound stood up, then another and another. Soon, a group of towering runners encircled George and peered quizzically down at the corgi.

"Explain!" demanded Griselda.

"You won't know this yet, but dogs and humans from another dimension called Earth are helping our true leader, Bosona, get rid of that imposter, Bruiser."

"Hoo-ray!" exclaimed Griselda. Nods and murmurings from the other greyhounds showed general agreement with the bitch, although whoever sat as Top Dog in the Great Hall was of minor importance to these champions of speed.

"Her new general, an Earth dog called Bouncer—"

"What a funny name!" interrupted one of the younger dogs, at which all, except Griselda, laughed again.

"Well, be that as it may, Bouncer wants to keep his Earth human here as a pet. Back there it's the other way around, you see. Humans keep dogs as pets." The hilarity of this had some of the greyhounds helplessly rolling around on the floor. But not Griselda.

"Hmm!" George understood he'd have to change tack if more than Griselda were to be persuaded.

"Greyhounds in Hawick win fortunes," he said, without having a clue why, for he reckoned it wasn't true, but the response was immediate. Stunned silence.

"Fortunes?" one of the hecklers queried.

"This human, the pet of our new general, is highly respected by dogs there. By which I mean greyhounds. She's definitely popular with greyhounds."

"Of course," agreed the heckler. "Right, friends? Hear that? Treats us greyhounds with the respect we deserve. Tell me—" He came up close to the corgi. "Tell me more about this dimension you call Hawick."

"Earth," interrupted George. "Hawick is somewhere on Earth. Part of a really important country called Scotland."

"Are greyhounds ever Top Dogs there?"

"So top that they even name buses after them. They have Greyhound buses in Scotland." He had overheard the professor talking to Dylan and Alice about his travels in the Americas way back and how these would have been far easier with Greyhound buses.

"Greyhound buses, guys. Named after us," the young dog repeated. "Um—what's a bus?"

"Good question, but I'm sure buses can't go as fast as you lot. Not even when they call them greyhounds. You see, guys, if you let this girl down, well, there's no telling what'll happen to the reputations of greyhounds in Hawick."

"Reputations, ay?"

"No reputations, no bets, guys! Think of your fellow greyhounds in Hawick." The greyhounds exchanged looks.

"When?" asked Griselda.

"As soon as you're ready. At the foot of the mountain. In relays of four teams, four apiece. That's sixteen of your fastest. Across the plain. No ambushes that way. Think you can outpace the bloodhounds?"

The lounge filled with renewed laughter, though, as he left, George heard the beginnings of arguments as to who would be the fastest across the plain to the coal house. On his way up the stairs he had the good fortune to meet the mongrels, Bill and Ben, who were also unhappy about Bouncer's plan to separate Alice from the other Hawick humans.

"Quick!" urged George. "Go straight to the coal house. Have the Vortex primed and ready. Won't have much time there even if the greyhounds can outrun the bloodhounds. You know what those big-nosed dogs are like. They just never give up."

Like the bloodhounds, the twins too had perseverance. And they could be trusted. The corgi lolloped up the stairs but stopped a few steps down from the landing of the door to the Tower. Something was happening up there. He held back...

***

"Wait!" yelled Dylan. The others froze and looked at him. "Put the duck—I mean Caitlin—inside the dress. In case she—you know. Can't have my sister with nothing on. Not when she's no longer a duck."

"Thank you for thinking of that," said Alice. Dylan grinned with pride. "We were all in too much of a hurry."

"Stop yakking. Ben, take the duck—I mean the girl—to where Rusty is." It was the professor and he sounded impatient. As if time was fast running out. "Have them both lying down, so their heads are touching. Make sure that little red tuft of hers gets mingled with his hair. And keep her calm. If she flaps her wings, all might be lost when I blow crystal dust over them. It's all to do with molecular transformation, you see. No magic involved."

"Professor—?" began Dylan.

"What?"

"I think my sister understood every word you said. Look at her eyes. The one facing us, at least." True. The duck's bright eye seemed to take in everything that was going on. She was obviously terrified and her wings most definitely would not flap.

Ben positioned the duck and ruffled Rusty's hair around the little red tufts sprouting from the head of the duck. The old man, after cutting at the empty air around the human-duck pair's heads, placed the scissors on the ground. Dylan and Alice transferred handfuls of crystal dust into the bony, cupped hands of Professor Pringle. Without losing a single fleck, he gently puffed this over the faces of Caitlin and the Dogtopian man, then, afterwards, over the rest of their bodies. Handful after handful were blown over man and duck until both were covered with a shimmering layer of golden yellow. Still nothing happened. George mounted the last few stairs and crept a little closer, worrying about what they would do if the human girl were to remain a duck. He knew full well that neither Bouncer nor Bosona would be able to resist a quick gulp of such a 'special' duck. Even he felt tempted.

Dylan scooped up what was left of the crystal dust off the floor and carefully sprinkled this into Alice's small palms. The Chinese girl, with the professor's permission, blew these last flecks over the duck's bill which had somehow remained dust-free. Still nothing happened. The boy from Hawick began to panic. Even if they were to return to Scotland, how on Earth could he hand his parents a duck and say, 'By the way, this is Caitlin.'?

"Shouldn't we now separate them?" suggested Alice.

"No, their molecules will be—" began the Professor.

"With the scissors, I mean," interrupted the girl. "They really are magical. I'm sure of it."

"Science," the professor tetchily insisted. "Only science."

"Whatever, they changed Scissorman."

"Alice is right," said Dylan. "So did my penknife. Perhaps—" He looked thoughtful. "Maybe something in the scissors from when you changed them will allow molecular information to be shared between Rusty and the duck. What Alice is trying to say is that perhaps they should be separated with the scissors for crystal to work. Maybe—"

"As he says," agreed Alice, and this time there was something more than admiration in her eyes. *Could it be?* Dylan silently prayed.

The professor mumbled, "Don't blame me if—" as Alice snipped across the hair-join between human and duck patiently waiting, head-to-head, on the ground. In a flash, Caitlin the girl reappeared, in her red dress, with her head up against the human's.

"Well—as you see it was only a matter of time," muttered Professor Pringle. "You Hawick folk are so impatient!" Caitlin immediately sat up and opened her mouth. For a few awful moments, Dylan thought she was going to quack, until...

"Where am I?" she asked.

Ben offered her his hand and she stood up. Rusty looked at the others.

"Aye!" he agreed. "Where am I the noo?" he added in a broad Scottish Borders accent.

Dylan and Alice burst into laughter.

"What's so funny?" asked Caitlin. "I've just spent the last twenty-four hours or so as a flipping duck and now you're laughing! Ugh! Brothers!"

"Caitlin, it's not you they're laughing at," said Ben. "It's Rusty. Not only can he now speak, but he's got a Hawick accent like you. Teri talk, ay? Hey, Rusty. Can you spell E-G-Y-P-T like a Hawick man?"

"Nothing wrong with Teri talk," Caitlin pouted. "Hey!" She'd just noticed Rusty staring at her red knickers and bra still lying on the ground. "D'you mind, mister?" She snatched them up. "All of you look away, please."

She slipped her underwear on underneath her dress whilst George became increasingly restless. Ben, meanwhile, asked Rusty why Tarzan, his Dogtopian human friend, had laughed at the sign of a cross. Rusty chuckled. Ben frowned.

"It means 'I've got a boyfriend already', ken. Women do it to us if they think we're getting too friendly."

"Oh—no wonder!" exclaimed Ben.

"Hey, that's not funny!" exclaimed Caitlin. "I just know that Ben isn't gay!"

George had had enough of time-wasting. "They'll be coming for you soon, Alice," he said.

"Who?" asked the Chinese girl, smiling so happily to see her wee neighbour human again.

"The bloodhounds. I was ordered to bring you to Bouncer. You're to stay here as his pet. Forever." Alice's smile vanished. "If I return with Rusty instead, I might just persuade him that's acceptable. Now that Rusty's talking. Unlikely, though. He says he needs *you* to help the professor here get other humans to talk."

"As humans used to long, long ago," added Professor Pringle. "But before that, I'll need to take Rusty back with me to South America if the crystal in the chest's all been used up."

Alice's mouth opened but she remained speechless.

"Look," said George, "I'll try my best to hold them back. Try to persuade Bouncer that Rusty will do as a substitute pet. But I doubt it'll work. He likes you too much, Alice. You'd better get down the mountain right now. Greyhound teams will take all four of you across the plain at top speed. I don't think the bloodhounds will stand a chance of catching up with them. Bill and Ben should be at the Vortex by now. Charging it up."

"I'm here," said Ben.

"Ben the mongrel," explained George.

"Ben's Chinese, not mongrel," Caitlin remarked indignantly.

Ben chuckled. "You mean Mongolian, Caitlin. And yes, my great grandmother did come from Outer Mongolia."

"Oh. Sorry."

"Don't be. It's so wonderful to have you back."

"Is it really?" Her bright blue eyes peered shyly up at the Chinese boy. "You're not just saying that?"

"Yes, it is. And as the Caitlin we love. Though you're not the only girl here we *all* love!" He winked at Dylan who glanced at Alice then blushed crimson.

"Get going, you lot! Down those stairs at top speed," urged George. "Out the side entrance, down the scree and onto those greyhounds at the bottom. One each."

"Wow!" exclaimed Caitlin. "We don't even *have* greyhounds in Hawick and I'm gonna ride on one!"

"The dogs think you do, Caitlin, so keep quiet about that," said George. "It's why they're helping you. Because of Hawick greyhounds being so important on Earth. And because of the Greyhound buses there."

"What?" queried Caitlin.

"Never mind! Alice is in terrible trouble. She's now the pet that Bouncer doesn't want to lose."

"Like when I was looking for him after he went missing?" suggested the Chinese girl.

"He loves you but couldn't say it. Not in front of Bosona. Now go!" insisted George.

"Let *me* do the talking in the Great Hall, George," proposed Professor Pringle. "Bosona might get Bouncer to see sense."

"Unlikely. I think she's still suffering from shock," George reckoned. "Certainly not her usual self."

"No way is my sister gonna stay here in Dogtopia," said Ben "Follow me. And hurry!"

Two Earth brothers and two Earth sisters fled down the stairs and out of the palace before scrambling down the scree to the plain below where four stream-lined greyhounds, bigger than large antelopes, were eagerly waiting, ready to take off on the race of his or her life. The four young neighbours from Hawick clambered onto their narrow backs and, like arrows shot from Dylan's discarded bow, they sped across the flat, open land. Not only were they competing against the threat of the bloodhounds, but the dogs seemed only too keen to race each other. Holding on for dear life, the teenagers wrapped their arms around the dogs' necks as they flew faster than the wind to the first relay where four more greyhounds stood poised for action like Olympic sprinters crouched on starting blocks.

Dylan looked back. Moving specks in the distance, approaching from Palace Mountain, confirmed that Bouncer had got his way. For whatever reason, he was clearly intent on Alice remaining in Dogtopia. Fresh greyhound mounts soon widened the gap between the youngsters from Hawick and the bloodhounds. When the boy glanced sideways, and saw the excitement written across his sister's now human and very pretty face, he decided that this was the second-best moment of his life to date. The best had been Alice resting her head on his shoulder.

Two mounts later and they arrived at the coal house. The door was open. Dylan didn't dare look back across the plain to see whether the bloodhounds had continued with the chase. Once inside, where Bill and Ben had the Vortex machine primed and ready to transport them back to Hawick, no time was wasted.

"Girls first," said Ben-the-boy. "Quick!"

Caitlin looked anxiously at Alice.

"It's okay," reassured the Chinese girl. "Just so long as we don't have another passenger like Dylan and I had. A mouse!"

"But—will I get turned back into a duck?"

Dylan knew they couldn't be sure. Duck, cat... dinosaur? His confidence in the professor's technological expertise, though not in Alice's ingenuity, had shrunk. But he trusted his neighbour to take good care of his little sister. The girls disappeared into the Vortex, Bill closed the lid with his paw and Ben-the-dog did his performing dog dance at the controls, tapping, pushing and pulling, with both front paws, at knobs, buttons and levers. The Vortex shook and trembled, as did Dylan's heart inside his chest. The hum reduced, slowly. It remained steady for a few moments then faded to nothing.

"Well done, Alice," he whispered.

"That's it?" asked Ben.

Dylan nodded. "She's made it," he replied.

"Well, you just tell that father of yours my sister isn't stupid," said the Chinese boy. Dylan glanced at his neighbour. "It's not *you*, Dylan. It's your father. I think—" Ben wore one of those wonderfully-open smiles that made the him so popular. "I think she really likes you, Dylan. She has to admit it to herself first, though."

Dylan shrugged his shoulders. Ben-the-dog tapped at a flashing green button and the Vortex lid flipped open again.

"You first, Dylan. You know how this thing works."

"Not really. I just—"

A burst of bangs on the coal house door caused the boys to freeze. A huge slavering dog face appeared at the window. Dylan could see why there was so much fuss about fox hunting back home. To be the quarry of those beasts would be terrifying.

"In! Now!" shouted Bill, who leapt to the window and bared his fangs at the bloodhounds. Dylan almost flew up the ladder. For a fleeting moment, he felt saddened to see the seats empty, for he so desperately wanted to be reunited with Caitlin and Alice in that faraway dimension of Earth. He dropped into one of these. Soon, Ben was strapped in beside him. Dylan reached for the lever where Whiskers, now safely back inside his rucksack, had become wedged. His hand gently caressed the brake as if it were Alice's arm. Masks dropped down.

"It's up to you now, friend!" whispered Ben, before pulling a mask over his face. "With Alice, I mean!" He must have read Dylan's mind.

The hum grew louder, the light brighter and they started to shake. Dylan kept his eyes tightly shut all the time. Like a seasoned expert, he eased back on the brake when the hum started to fade. Everything went quiet. He remained still, eyes closed, fearing the worst. The lid sprang open.

Which dimension? What time period?

"You first, pilot!" said Ben.

How can he still smile like that? God, suppose I've taken him back to the time of the Romans? What would they make of a Chinese boy? Guess they did know about Chinese silk, though, what with the Silk Road and all...

"Dylan?"

"Sorry, Ben. Just that—if it's Saturday—d'you think she'll still want to go and see Colin play rugby?"

"Like I said, it's up to you, dude. Come on! Let's get out of this contraption."

Up to me?

Dylan stood. He popped his head out of the Vortex. Scottie looked up from the controls.

"Welcome to Dinoland!" he joked, but Dylan did not find it funny. And where were Caitlin and Alice?

"Where are they?" he anxiously asked as he eased himself out. Ben followed.

"Who?" asked Scottie.

"The elephants!" joked Ben. Dylan looked at him. Sometimes he just couldn't understand the Chinese boy's humour, and this was one of those moments. Ben was struggling to suppress the giggles.

"What?" queried Dylan. He peered over his shoulder. Up popped Caitlin. She and Alice had been crouching down, hidden from view. Caitlin now dangled an arm from her face and proceeded to trumpet like an elephant.

"Miss Caitlin Ross, I do believe you are destined for a career in Hollywood. As an elephant!" said Ben.

"I think she'd prefer to play the heroine," said Dylan.

"Only if Ben's the lead actor," added Caitlin.

Despite the hug he got from Alice, Dylan still worried about Colin.

"What day is it here?" he asked Scottie.

"Saturday, of course."

"Time?"

"Same as when you first entered the Vortex."

"Oh!"

"Better get you home, sis," Ben said to Alice.

"Wait!" the Chinese girl exclaimed. She approached Dylan. *Shall I tell her how I feel? Ben, help me please!* He turned his face sideways hoping for at least a kiss on the cheek. "He's still in your rucksack," she said instead of kissing him.

"Who?" *If only I could shove Colin in there!* thought Dylan.

"Whiskers! You put him back in the rucksack. Inside your hankie. After Caitlin got changed back. Don't you remember?"

"Oh—of course! Silly me!"

He slipped off his rucksack, opened it and—

"Hello!" hailed a squeaky little voice. Dylan dropped the rucksack. "Ouch!" it cried out.

Alice knelt to retrieve Whiskers. She stroked him, and Dylan squatted beside her.

"I'm so sorry," he said, more for Alice's benefit than Whiskers'. "I mean—I'd never heard a rucksack say 'hello' before. Got a shock. That's all." Thankfully Alice laughed, and her laugh was just like her brother's.

"Hear that, Whiskers? You gave my neighbour a shock," she said.

Why can't she say boyfriend instead of neighbour? thought Dylan.

"I got hungry, and there was all this gold dust lying around. The place was dark, but the dust glowed. And it smelt tasty," squeaked the mouse.

"Oh Dylan, you went and left some of the dust behind! Now we've got a talking mouse on our hands."

"You'll need a new pet, I'm thinking," the boy said.

Alice's eyes lit up—then looked troubled. "A mouse that squeaks and speaks?"

"Hey, you guys! You talking about me, by any chance?"

"Can I hold him?" asked Caitlin.

"Look, I am not a toy! I need to get back home. To my wife and kids," squeaked Whiskers.

"Where?" asked Alice.

"The old house. Got picked up by some stupid dog. Escaped in that big tub thing and hid till you guys found me.

I was so glad you weren't dogs. Never did like dogs. Or cats. Prefer humans." For a moment, Dylan remembered how, because of Poppy the Poodle, Alice was nearly turned into a barking human. Alice looked at Dylan. He couldn't quite work out the meaning behind that look.

"I think I prefer humans too," she agreed. "Do you still want to be a vet, Dylan?"

"Not so sure now," he replied.

"Come up to Edinburgh in the Autumn," Ben suggested. "I'll show you around the medical school. Who knows? Perhaps Alice and I could persuade you to become a doctor instead?"

Alice wants me to be a doctor? Dylan turned pink. He was beginning to feel like a chameleon with his face constantly changing colour in the Chinese girl's presence.

"Can I come as well?" asked Caitlin.

"Sure! Wouldn't be the same without our beautiful red-haired neighbour!" said Ben. "All four of us can get together again. Have lunch somewhere. Plus, I've got to get those shoes for you, sis."

"Ben—oh, thank you! You are awesome!" Alice gave her brother another hug.

"You could all take the train up from Galashiels."

"Hear that, Dylan? We're going to Edinburgh by train! Wow!" fizzed Caitlin.

"Ahem! If you don't mind, I need to get home," Whiskers reminded them.

They followed Scottie out of the coal house, across the unkempt garden, through the back door, the kitchen and into the hallway of Number Twenty-four.

"This'll do," said Whiskers, peering over the edge of Alice's hand. She gently lowered him to the ground. Dylan's heart now raced. *Now or never,* he reckoned. *Kick-off at 2.00 pm.*

They bid Scottie goodbye, each wondering whether they'd ever again meet a talking dog. At the Ross's gate, they parted. Dylan finally plucked up courage to call out to Alice:

"Alice, are you—um—?" But the rest of the sentence remained stuck in his brain.

"No, I am *not* barking mad!" she replied, and Ben laughed.

"Thank goodness," Dylan said. "No, it's not that. It's about... I mean... rugby? Will you be, you know—?"

"Know what?" The Chinese girl looked puzzled. She walked back to where Dylan and his sister stood. Dylan's heart raced like a Dogtopian greyhound.

"What my brother means is would you prefer to see his train set than watch Colin play rugby?" interjected Caitlin.

Dylan turned a deep shade of beetroot. "I don't have a train set, Caitlin," he said, frowning.

"I know, but Alice doesn't!"

Dylan wasn't prepared for what happened next. The Chinese girl, still grinning, kissed him on the cheek.

"No rugby," she whispered. "Prefer trains!"

"Come on, sis," said Ben. "I'm starving. That dog food was awful!" He slipped his hand into his pocket and took out Caitlin's red brooch. "Here, have it back. It belongs to you. Just wasn't happy in my pocket. And if you'd been wearing this, maybe it would never have happened."

Caitlin ran to Ben and took the brooch, turning it over thoughtfully a few times. As she and Dylan watched their neighbours disappear back into the Changs' house, Dylan asked his sister:

"D'you think I stand a chance? You're a girl. You should know." Caitlin gave her brother a playful punch in the ribs.

"Actually, I don't think Colin has a hope in hell of beating my big brother this time!"

"But *how*? What should I do?" Dylan asked.

"Just tell her the truth. Oh, I wish I wasn't so young. Then I could tell Ben how much I love him!"

"You'll grow up."

"Aye—plus he's gonna find Miss Wonderful at uni even before I leave school."

"Like I said, you'll grow up, Caitlin. But not too fast, please. I do like having a little sister around."

"Hmm! Boiled egg, big brother?"

"What?"

"Being a duck made me think about eggs. I could die for a boiled egg for breakfast."

Die? Please don't!

Arm-in-arm, brother and sister re-entered a home which, for a while, in a strange dimension of talking dogs, both thought they would never again see.

***

"I'm so sorry I shouted at her, son."

Dylan, standing at the window of his bedroom, and peering down at the garden next door, turned to face his father.

"It's Alice you should apologise to. Not me," he said. He looked again at the girl who had changed his life in such a profound way that things would never again be the same. Dressed in a red top and short blue skirt, she sat alone on a swing that hadn't been used for years, gently rocking herself to-and-fro, lost in another world. Dylan wished he was privy to her thoughts. Was she thinking about Bouncer whom she

187

would never see again, or was she wishing that it had been Colin McPhail with those rugger-powered muscles, instead of him, who had accompanied her to a land where humans and dogs had reversed roles?

Thank God she escaped from her 'owner', but what on earth is on her mind? the boy wondered.

Mr Ross came up to stand beside Dylan. He rested a hand on his son's shoulder.

"She's a really nice girl," he said. "And very bright indeed." Dylan glanced sideways at his father with an anger that seemed neither able to show itself nor hold back. He felt confused.

"I've an idea," Mr Ross said. "You may not agree, but I'll be happy to help out in any way I can." Dylan didn't like his father's ideas if they involved upsetting the only girl, apart from his sister, whom he really cared about. "First, you and I need to talk."

"Talk then," said Dylan tetchily. "I'm not leaving this window." And so, as father and son watched the girl on the swing, Mr Ross explained how he came by his limp.

"I was your age," he said. "As you know, we lived in Edinburgh. Semi-detached. A quiet street. One summer, a family moved in next door. Two boys. Not my type. Older and forever getting into trouble. They had a dog which they never played with. A mongrel. You won't believe this, but I loved animals back then. And the mongrel made up for those tearaway brothers who ignored me anyway. He was called Jimbo. We became great friends, and whenever I came home from school, Jimbo would be at his front gate waiting for me. Wagging his tail."

Dylan pictured a horse sized Jimbo similar to Bill and Ben, the Dogtopian mongrels.

"The day it happened was a Saturday. The boys had gone to the park to play soccer, they said. If only I'd known what they'd just done. It was a lovely day. Bright and sunny. I summoned the courage to go and ask if I could take Jimbo for a walk. Occasionally the boys' father took the poor dog out at night, but Jimbo rarely saw daylight."

Dylan couldn't see where this was heading. He just wanted to go down and talk to Alice, if only to share reminiscences about another dimension in a coal house at the back of Number Twenty-four.

"The door was answered by Mrs Craigie. A tiny slip of a woman who was terrified of her law-breaking sons. If I'd known that those bastards had just tried to squeeze Jimbo into the washing machine for a prank that very morning, moments earlier, I'd not have rung the bell."

Dylan looked at his Dad, the anger gone. He sensed what was coming and it frightened him.

"Jimbo—barking like he'd gone rabid—jumped at me and grabbed my leg between his jaws." Mr Ross tapped at his limping leg. "This one. I lost my balance and fell. Mrs Craigie only screamed. She made no attempt to pull him off. I should have hit Jimbo but couldn't. I could never hit an animal. Also—" Mr Ross paused. His hand dropped from Dylan's shoulder and he ran both hands through his hair, as if this might give him strength to continue the painful recollection. Dylan felt overwhelmed by guilt for never having asked his dad how he came by the limp about which he, Dylan, got teased at school. "The neck. Like most carnivores, dogs go for the neck. My instinct was to protect my neck with both hands. Like this." He held both hands up to his neck as if to save it from being torn open by unseen giant jaws. "But Jimbo wasn't going to let go of my leg. I felt something break when he twisted it in both directions. I—"

Dylan reached back and hugged his father close to him. Of late, neither had shown any degree of physical familiarity towards the other. The boy thought that even if Alice were to choose Colin, this whole business had given him a better understanding of the man who had played such a vital part in giving him life.

"Must have passed out," his father continued. "Next thing I knew I was in an ambulance with the siren blaring. A passing motorist had saved my life. I was in hospital for three months. Had a serious infection. *Very* serious."

So now Dylan understood the man's obsession about bugs from animals.

"But for a new antibiotic that had just come out, I'd have lost a leg. And maybe my life. There was one compensation, though. The physiotherapist was very pretty." Mr Ross looked down at the girl in the swing. "Like Alice." He winked at his son. "Which brings me to my suggestion. It'll mean extra work for you, of course."

Dylan guessed what was coming. His confidence tree began to show signs of recovery. It had grown to the size of the apple tree in the Changs' garden.

"Give Alice private maths coaching?" he queried.

His dad nodded.

"With my blessing. As her maths teacher. Look, I meant it when I said she's really bright. But I have this theory that she has dyscalculia." Dylan frowned. It sounded like some awful disease and looking at her now she looked so perfectly healthy. "Similar to dyslexia," continued Mr Ross senior. "Just for arithmetic and algebra. She's better than you at geometry."

"Oh! Really?" That's all Dylan could say, but his grin stretched from one ear to the other. He left the window.

"Where are you going?" his dad asked.

The boy halted at the door.

"To tell her," he replied.

"To *ask* her, Dylan! Not tell. See if she'd like to come round. You're right. It's Alice I must apologise to. But I also want to discuss a new program I've worked out for kids suffering from dyscalculia. With both of you."

Dylan chuckled.

"You want Alice to be your guinea pig?" A corner of the boy's brain conjured a world run by giant guinea pigs. The squeaks would be deafening, unless, like Dogtopian dogs, they were able to speak instead of squeak.

"I only wish you to be happy, son," Mr Ross said. "And that vet business? You know, it's what I always wanted to be before the accident."

"Hardly an accident, Dad. What happened to Jimbo, by the way?"

"Put down. I felt bad about that, too. I think the poor dog might've got over his shock. Just that I turned up at the wrong time. Look, seeing Alice down there so sad—I think this might be the right time for you to talk to her."

Dylan ran down the stairs two at a time. He ran to the Changs' house and rang the bell. No reply. Of course! She'd be on her own in the garden. Ben and Mr Chang would be practising *tai chi* in the park and Mrs Chang gave Chinese classes in the church hall some Saturdays. If it hadn't been for the confidence his dad had infused into him, he might have returned home and sulked for the rest of the day. Instead he pushed open the small gate to the back garden and ran, like a Dogtopian greyhound, along the path. Alice looked up from the swing.

"Dylan!" she exclaimed, but her smile said so much more.

"Woof woof!" replied Dylan. Alice laughed. She jumped up and ran to him. He wasn't prepared for what happened next. She flung her arms around him and hugged him close. When they'd separated, she kept hold of his hands.

"I'm so sorry!" they both said at the same time, then giggled.

"Dad wants to apologise," Dylan told her. "Personally, like. To you." Alice gave the boy a soft playful punch.

"My teacher wants to say 'sorry'? But he was right. Bouncer wasn't who I thought he was."

"Bouncer didn't want to lose you. That was the problem." His tree was still too small to add, 'Neither do I. Not to that ape Colin McPhail'. "No, it's not about Bouncer. Something else. But first I must tell you about Dad's limp."

And so, with Alice rocking herself backwards and forwards on the swing, and Dylan sitting at her feet on the grass, the girl learned how her maths teacher once came close to death after being savaged by a dog.

"Oh, your poor dad," she said, tears brimming her eyes. "And I've been so mean about him. Like all the others at school. No! *I* should say sorry!"

"Whatever," continued Dylan, "but he's come up with a plan. For your maths!"

"Oh, not that! Please!"

"Apparently, you've got this thing with a posh name that means it's hard for you to do arithmetic and stuff."

"No need to rub it in! I'm thick! Can hardly call that a posh word."

"You are *not!* You've just got this posh-named—um—sort of condition."

"What condition?"

Dylan didn't like to say it sounded like a disease.

"Dys— something or other. And people who have this are particularly intelligent in other areas."

"Like knowing who to kiss?"

Dylan laughed.

"Absolutely! No Colins! But there's a downside, hen."

"Tell me, dude! I have to go back to primary school, right?"

"You have to get private coaching from yours truly."

"That geek Dylan Ross?"

Dylan gave the girl a playful slap on the knee.

"Did you know this is the year of the dog for us Chinese? Even in Hawick."

"That figures," said Dylan. "But more like the year of the 'no dog' for Alice Chang, ay?"

"I ken. But I've got something much, much better instead."

"What? A rabbit or something?"

Alice looked at Dylan in a funny way.

"Better looking than a rabbit."

"I'll never let you down! Not like Bouncer. I promise. Look, Dad's got this new teaching program. For people with dys—... whatever it's called. And it'll be supervised by our head of maths!"

"Who happens to be your dad! Will my parents have to pay?"

"Ah! There's the rub, lass! No exchange of money. I get a hug after every lesson instead."

"Sounds good to me. When can we start?"

Dylan looked at his watch.

"Two minutes from here to my place. Last one through our front door is a nerd!" Alice leapt from the swing and was running along the passage before Dylan could lift himself up off the grass.

Perhaps Colin should give me private running lessons, he thought.

Alice's first lesson from her new tutor, alone in his bedroom, took rather longer than Mr Ross anticipated.

"I hope the program isn't too hard for her," he said to Ben when the Chinese boy turned up at the Ross's front door wondering whether Alice was with Dylan. Without knocking, Ben opened the door to Dylan's room, thankfully blocking the view for Dylan's dad. Alice and Dylan sprang apart and exchanged guilty looks. Ben, as always, saved the day:

"Oh, I'm sure they've had plenty of other things to talk about as well, Mr Ross," he said, looking over his shoulder. "Right, sis?" The older boy's wink was like super-fertilizer for Dylan's confidence tree. This time it promised to outgrow the largest-ever Californian redwood.

"Where's the house, Mummy?" the child asked. Her pretty eyes were Chinese, like her mother's, but her light brown hair was that of her father. Alice Ross glanced at her husband, uncertain how much more they should tell their daughter about a journey that brought them together twelve years back. "And why didn't you get another dog after you lost Bouncer?"

The child's mother looked the other way without replying. Detouring through the Scottish Borders on the long drive from London to Aberdeen had not been her idea.

"We'll show you the house. But promise me you'll never go inside," said Dylan, Jemmy's dad.

"Honestly, I don't think we should, Dylan." Alice, who so nearly became trapped forever as a human pet of her beloved dog in the strangest land imaginable, looked troubled.

"It's her past as well as ours, honey," her husband pointed out. "But for Bouncer getting lost, she might not even exist. She has a right to know everything. Better she does to give her strength if ever she meets—"

The man wasn't sure how to put into words something that had hovered in his mind since speeding back with his then-classmate-now-wife, his sister and his brother-in-law, on the backs of giant greyhounds, across the wide and empty plain of Dogtopia...

Scissorman!

"Meet who, Daddy?"

"I really don't think this is a good idea," warned Alice.

Somehow, she always felt safe with Dylan. Finally, although reluctant, she had agreed to see Hawick again before driving on up to the Highlands for a well-earned summer holiday, and to meet up with Jemmy's much-loved Uncle Ben.

They parked in the street of their childhood. Alice's parents had moved up north to be near their son, a doctor in the Aberdeen Royal Infirmary, whilst Dylan, also a doctor, worked down in London. His sister, Caitlin, a promising actress, lived in Los Angeles. She had never quite got over 'losing' Ben to a 'silly nurse' in Aberdeen. At least, Caitlin claimed she must be silly though she had never met the girl. And she consoled herself with the thought that Ben had not, as yet, married 'Miss Silly'.

All their lives were blown apart when Dylan's and Caitlin's parents were killed in a car crash. That's when Alice and Dylan decided to get married. Their marriage shone like a torch in that darkness of death and despair. And Dylan gave Caitlin his share of their inheritance to help her acting career.

"That's where Aunty Caitlin and I lived," Dylan said to wee Jemmy, pointing to his old house. "The home of the notorious maths teacher," he added grinning at Alice.

"What's notorious mean?"

"Famous?" suggested the girl's mother. "And your grandfather was a lovely man. Daddy's only teasing."

"Famous for getting you through your maths exams, ay?"

"You did that, Mr Dylan Ross!"

"And you and Uncle Ben lived in the house next door, Mummy? With the red door?"

"Aye."

"Red was a lucky colour. For me!" added Dylan.

"So... where's Number Twenty-four?"

Alice frowned. Taking his wife and daughter by the hand, Dylan led them around the corner.

A large 'For Sale' sign had been planted in the garden of Number Twenty-four, so overgrown now that the front door was barely visible. All the windows that could be seen were boarded up.

"Do you think he'll ever come back?" Alice asked quietly.

"The professor? Who knows?"

"Not the professor. I trusted him. No, I was referring to Scissorman. Even if the Vortex has gone, there's still that room upstairs. Where I thought I'd lost Ben forever."

"Uncle Ben told me about that room. Connected to the Interim, he said. What is the Interim?" asked Jemmy.

"No good asking me. I'm only a doctor."

"Daddy... what's that dark shadow over there? Moving about behind that tree? The one with the funny red eyes?"

For a few moments the child's parents stared in horror but saw nothing. Dylan knew Jemmy, like himself, was always truthful.

"Back to the car! Run!" he shouted.

They didn't stop running till they had reached the car. That's when he saw it. In the windscreen mirror. A dark shape with long arms and searching spaghetti-like fingers, floating at speed towards them. Jemmy giggled as he turned on the engine, slammed the accelerator and swerved the car off up the road. Warning lights flashed. Only Jemmy had her seat belt buckled. Alice, in shock, sat rigid with fear.

"Buckle-up, Alice!" said Dylan, fixing his seat-belt as he drove on.

Screeching around corners, the car zig-zagged out of town, only slowing down as they passed the police headquarters.

"Hey, this is fun!" shrieked Jemmy.

"Not if he catches up with us it won't be," said Dylan. He glanced in the mirror. Thankfully they were no longer being followed.

"You really do need those special scissors of Mummy's unless you want to be turned into a duck," Jemima piped up. "If he does."

"Does what?"

"Catch you up."

"How do you know about—?"

"Uncle Ben told me," interrupted the child.

"What?"

"He's got them. In Aberdeen."

"The Scissors?"

They drove on in silence until reaching a layby. Dylan pulled in and turned off the engine. With Alice in tears, he turned to address their daughter.

"What are you saying, Jemima? This is no joking matter."

"Uncle Ben said not to tell you. Not before. He went back there to get them. In case."

"In case of what?"

The girl shrugged her shoulders.

"That's all he said. 'In case'. Can I have an ice cream when we get to Innerleithen? You did say."

"That sounds a very good idea to me, Miss Jemima Ross." Alice was still in tears. Dylan hugged her, then, *taking a detour to confuse Scissorman, drove on towards the promised ice cream. "And when we get to Aberdeen, we'll get those scissors. I guess Ben reckoned we'd not need them down in London."*

Alice rested her head on her husband's shoulder until they pulled up outside the ice cream shop which, Jemmy had been informed, made the best ice cream in Scotland.

"Don't worry, Mummy," said Jemmy. "Uncle Ben has it all sorted. He knows what to do."

"What?" her mother asked.

"Easy!" answered Jemmy. "Cut his head off. After snipping his fingers."

Dylan chuckled.

"Easy, ay?" he queried.

"Yes. For you it is, Daddy."

Alice smiled and took hold of her husband's hand.

"I agree," she said. "Come on. Let's have that ice cream!"

The Author

Oliver Eade, born a Londoner, now an adopted Scot, retired from a career in hospital medicine thinking 'feet up and watch the telly', but this wasn't to be. After waking up one night with a ghost story in his head, he took to writing adult short stories. Over fifty have been published, several winning prizes, and many appear in a collection, **Walls of Words**. His first young readers' book, **Moon Rabbit**, a magical journey to Mythological China (Oliver's wife is Chinese), was published in 2009. It was a winner of the Writers' and Artists' 2007 New Novel Competition and long-listed for the Waterstones Children's 2008 Book Prize. The sequel, **Monkey King's Revenge**, came out in 2011 and was a children's genre finalist for the 2012 People's Book Prize. **Northwards**, a young readers' dark fantasy based in Texas and the Arctic, was first published in 2010. **The Rainbow Animal**, a fun spoof on war for young and old readers, is also set in North America where Oliver's two eldest granddaughters live.

His debut adult novel, **A Single Petal**, which won the Local Legend 2012 Spiritual Writing Competition, is set in Tang Dynasty China (Local Legend Press). **Voices**, an adult novel of family love, intrigue and deceit, is set in London whilst the dark futuristic novel, **The Parth Path**, is set in a post-apocalyptic Scotland run by women for women. **The Terminus**, Oliver's debut young adult novel, returns to the city in which he was brought up: London, changed beyond recognition from the drab post-World War II era and which, in a post-apocalyptic world, gives Mankind a second chance. The **From Beast to God** trilogy, **The Golden**

Jaguar of the Sun, ***The Merging*** and ***Revelation***, follows a Texan boy and Mexican girl on a life-journey involving drug gangsters, ancient Aztec, Mayan and Native Mythology, blending European and Native American beliefs. ***The Kelpie's Eyes***, was inspired by a visit to the famous Scottish waterfall, the Grey Mare's Tale, and weaves Scottish mythology into a tale of sisterly love. It won the 2018 Georgina Hawtrey-Woore Young Adult Novel Award.

Oliver has also written several plays, one of which, ***The Gap***, inspired by being caught up in the Great Sichuan Earthquake of 2008, went on tour in Scotland in 2012. Another, ***The Other Cat***, a darkly humorous take on Schrödinger's famous feline, won the 2018 Segora International One Act Play Competition.

Although not confined to any particular genre, Oliver feels most comfortable in that magical space between reality and fantasy; the space into and out of which children slip so easily in their play; the place of dreams and myths and legends and deeply ingrained in many cultures across the globe.

Websites:
https://www.olivereadebooks.org
www.olivereade.co.uk
https://oddproductionstheatre.weebly.com

Contact: *olivereade@googlemail.com*

For other Silver Quill Publishing books for adults, teenagers and young readers, please visit: *www.silverquillpublishing.com*